Voyage To Freedom

VOYAGE TO FREEDOM

★

A Story of the Atlantic Crossing, 1620

★

David Gay

Illustrated by
Sandra Evans

THE BANNER OF TRUTH TRUST

THE BANNER OF TRUTH TRUST
3 Murrayfield Road, Edinburgh EH12 6EL, UK
P.O. Box 621, Carlisle, PA 17013, USA

*

© David Gay 1984
First published 1984
Reprinted 2004
Reprinted 2007

ISBN-10: 0 85151 384 0
ISBN-13: 978 0 85151 384 3

*

Scripture quotations are from the
Holy Bible, New International Version,
© International Bible Society 1978.

Printed in the U.S.A. by
Versa Press, Inc.,
East Peoria, IL

Contents

Introduction

You are standing on a narrow quayside waiting to board a small sailing ship. You are about to make an exciting but dangerous and uncomfortable voyage. I want you to pause, just for a moment or two. There are a few things I want you to know about the story of the voyage you are about to take. I want you to have a look at the little ship, its passengers and crew, and I want you to know the reason for making such a journey.

The first thing I want you to know is that the story is true. That is, it is based on historical fact. It tells the exciting story of the historic voyage of the 100 or so Pilgrims who crossed the Atlantic ocean in 1620. Master Reynolds, John Howland and William Butten all existed. It is a true story.

But, of course, we do not have a detailed record of all that went on during the voyage. We do not know all that was said. I have tried to weave a story around four imaginary characters – the Lovelace family – to show what the voyage must have been like. It happened very much as I have tried to show it.

The voyage was hard – very hard and very, very dangerous. I have tried to show you how hard a time the Pilgrims had. The ship was very tiny. The QE2, for example, is 66,000 tons. The *Mayflower* was only 180 tons. If you can imagine 6 or 7 family cars parked nose to tail – that is how long (or short) she was – and only about 4 cars wide! And yet she carried 100 passengers and 20 or so crew. A crossing of the Atlantic in recent times would only take a few days – the

Mayflower took 9 weeks! The passengers were crammed into a very tiny wooden sailing ship without proper rooms, food, air, beds or sanitation. It must have been horrible! They passed through storms. They were cheated and abused. They were blown off course.

Nor must we forget that it was a tremendous risk to take. They left their familiar and friendly homes and crossed the ocean to a new, unknown and dangerous land. Remember, the longest journey most people undertook in those days was less than 30 miles from their homes – and at the speed of a horse. The Pilgrims sailed 3000 miles!

Why did they do it?

The Pilgrims were Puritans. They wished to worship God simply – no special buildings – no special robes – no candles – no altars – no prayer books. They wished to worship God according to the way he had told them in his Word, the Bible. To do this, they had to leave England. The laws of the land, at that time, would not allow them to worship God according to the Bible and their conscience. They put God and his Word first in their lives – before their comfort or safety. They would endure anything and everything to obey God's laws.

God did not fail them. He protected them and took them safely to their new home. In such a voyage in those days, it was very common for many of the passengers to die. Not one of the Pilgrims died. In fact, one – Oceanus – was born during the crossing.

And now, the story is in front of you. I hope you enjoy it. I hope you feel something of the fears and hopes of young Justice and Prudence. I hope you learn of the God the story speaks of. May we all be true Pilgrims!

Fare you well, as you embark on this great adventure.

1 *Getting Ready*

IT was the August of 1620. The water front at Southampton was alive with the bustle and chatter of men carrying stores aboard the little rowing boats tied alongside. Boats already filled with the rope-tied chests and battered boxes were making their way out into the bay to two ships anchored

there. Some were already alongside and sailors, straining on the ropes, were pulling their precious cargoes out of the rowing boats and up on to the decks of the sea-going vessels.

The men carrying the cargoes to the rowing boats had to pass a sailor who checked their loads against a list fluttering in his hand. There were barrels and studded chests; mysterious bundles of every shape and size; salt and salt beef; cheese and dried peas, nails and screws; hammers; saws, axes and muskets; biscuits and drinking water; coils of rope and barrels of tar; squawking chickens and grunting squealing pigs; snapping dogs straining at their leash. The list must have seemed endless and so did the trail of dusty-mouthed and tired-limbed men winding its way back along the quay. The human snake twisted its tortuous way to the top of the well-worn, rickety and dripping steps and down on to the waiting rowing boats, as they bobbed up and down upon the water. Tall toppling houses pressed towards the sea from the town, vying with one another to see which could lean the furthest over the narrow quay before casting themselves and their occupants into the deep. There was little room on the narrow wharf at the best of times – and this certainly was not one of those. The cobbled jetty teemed with humanity.

Out in the bay, the *Speedwell* and the *Mayflower* pulled at their anchors in the rising tide. Seagulls wheeled about them, screaming as they dipped to the water. The breeze fluttered the colourful flags of the ships, and their wild flapping added to the general din. All was a blur of colour and a racket of yapping, snapping dogs, creaking carts and hollering men. The air was heavy with the smell of salt and stale fish.

Two old sailors with faces like weathered walnuts, worn brown with years of gazing into sun and salt sea, were leaning over the rail overlooking the quay. They stood with a knot of idling sailors, too old to put to sea again, who were wasting their time away as they watched the hive of activity below them. Men, women, children, soldiers and sailors were crushed together with dozens of dogs, goats and pigs all crowded on to the tiny cobbled quay.

'Where are the ships making for?' said one sailor, his walnut face cracking as he spoke.

'Virginia,' his friend replied with croaky voice.

'Wherever's that?' asked the first.

'It's one of the colonies in America.'

'Why ever is that speck of a ship going all that way?' snorted his friend as he pointed to the smaller of the two seagoing vessels. '*Speedwell* – is that her name?' he went on. 'I should say that's a good name for that ship. *Speedwell* indeed.' He slapped the back of his friend and his remark drew a guffaw of agreement from the others. 'She won't be going at speed to America, if I know anything about the sea. I reckon she'll do well enough to get past Land's End. Her mast is far too big if you ask me, and – look – she's carrying far too many sails for that small hull, I know. No!' he said aggressively, but no one was in a mind to oppose him, 'she'll never get that lot to Virginia. The *Mayflower*, the other'un, she looks more like it, but not that *Speedwell*.' After a pause he continued with a wondering sound to his voice. 'Anyway it's very strange. I can't take it in. It beats me. Why ever is it – that a bunch of Dutch people are coming to Southampton – to set sail to go all that way? Why do they want to live over the seas? Haven't they got enough room in Holland?'

'They aren't Dutch,' replied his crony. 'You know they're English.'

'But didn't I hear they've come from Leyden?'

'Aye, that's right enough but I tell you they're English. You know it's that so-called group of Pilgrims that want to go and settle in America. They're the ones who've hired the vessels.'

A shaky arm with pointed finger was raised towards the *Speedwell* again. 'I still say that that *Speedwell* will never get there. You mark my words,' said he, with a most definite ring to his voice. 'She's rigged all wrong. Anyway, you know who the captain is, don't you?' He didn't wait for an answer but carried on over a chorus of 'Ayes'. 'Yes, that's right,' said he with a smile on his leathery cheeks and a knowing nod. 'It's that Master Reynolds. You can guess his game, can't you? You can reckon he's up to no good. He'll have made a pretty penny out of the Pilgrims. A Pilgrim's gold is as good as any to him, you can be sure of that. Holy gold or wicked – 'twill make no difference.' This brought another laugh from the sailor band about him.

'Well, I don't know all about that,' came the reply, 'but I do know they're trying to get to Virginia. They say they want to set up their homes over there and they want more of their friends to come to them from Holland. That's the story so far as I've heard tell.'

'Why do they want to go to America to live? You say they're English – why ever can't they set up here then? If they're English what were they doing in Leyden in the first place? What are folks coming to these days, I say.'

'Matey, I explained that to you just now,' said his friend somewhat losing his patience. 'They're Pilgrims.' He took on his best schoolmaster air, plucked at the fingers of his left hand with the forefinger of his right, making his points of argument as he proceeded. 'You see, they say they want to worship God in the way that they see in the Bible. They want to worship God in a simple way. They don't believe the way we've been told is right. They're against the ways our laws tell 'em to worship and they want to go and live somewhere else where they can be free to do as they feel right. That's why they went to Holland in the first place. But now they want to live in their own country. They want to run their own affairs. They say they want to be free to worship God as they see in the Bible. D'you get it, now? You must have seen 'em carrying their great Bibles about. Surely you've heard all the talk they make about their conscience? Haven't you heard them making their speeches about living according to the Bible and in the light of their conscience and suchlike?'

4

'Conscience!' the second man interrupted, not liking to be treated as a naughty child who had failed to learn his lessons. 'Conscience! They must be fools and fanatics.' This drew another bout of back slapping and gaffaws from the crowd. 'And they've made a bad mistake all right in taking on that Master Reynolds, you mark my words. He'll lighten their pockets. If the English Pilgrims try to sail to America in that *Speedwell* they're heading for a watery grave. She'll never get there, you mark my words. She'll never get there.'

Just then, a tall, lean man came striding down the quay, making his way through the thronging crowd. Although the crowd was thick and noisy, the man had such a manner about him that he easily made his way through the throng. He gently pushed aside the people hindering him, until he stood at the head of the steps leading to the rowing boats. He was a fine, upright man with a clean-shaven face and a strong, pointed chin. He had a bright sparkle in his clear eyes. He had a serious manner about him and a determined look to his mouth. Even his clothes fitted his bearing for he wore no gaudy tunic. He was most plainly dressed in a simple black cloak. His legs, covered with tight dark stockings, suddenly disappeared into short black boots. Towering above his head stood a tall, wide-brimmed black hat. His hair, so short compared to the long curly manes of the sailors, poked neatly just beneath his hat. Around his neck he had a spotless white collar and in his hand he carried a large, smooth-worn, black leather book.

At his side, standing up to the level of his shoulder, stood a lady, also very plainly dressed. She wore a long flowing apron, pure white, that almost reached to her ankles. This apron rode over the soft folds of a neat black dress that covered her arms and peeped below the apron, just above her tiny black shoes. Her head was covered with a snow-white cap that hid all her hair. Her face shone, highlighted by the surrounding whiteness of her cap. Her tender eyes were alive with excitement. Her worn hands were clasped tightly before her.

Just behind the parents, two children were eagerly chattering to each other. When they stopped their chatter for a moment, they still held their mouths wide open, drinking in all they could see. They seemed to be lost in the seething mass of legs about them. They were in danger of being dragged away by the crowd and trampled. They kept their position by their parents only by their strong clutching grip upon their mother's fulsome skirts. The children were dressed, like their parents, in plain simple clothes of hard-wearing fustian with peeping white collars and cuffs.

The Pilgrims seemed to be all black and white. The only colour about them was the pale pink of their faces as they shone out in brilliance against the sombre background of their clothes.

One of the children pointed wildly at the ships. They hugged themselves, screwing themselves tight in their tingling excitement. They were agog with the thrill of it all.

The man stepped up to the sailor who held the cargo list in his hand.

'Matthew Lovelace,' he said, in a deep voice, addressing his remark to the sailor and raising his hand briefly to the brim of his hat. 'Matthew Lovelace, lately of Leyden in Holland, formerly of Scrooby in Nottinghamshire. Have my belongings been sent aboard the *Speedwell* yet, may I ask?'

The sailor with the cargo list ran his eye over the paper in front of him. 'Lovelace,' he drawled slowly. 'Lovelace, let me see.' He spoke wearily. Long hours had he spent at his post and his hot tired feet and aching legs called to him for eagerly awaited rest. At last he jabbed his finger at the list and ran it along an imaginary line. 'Yes sir,' came the reply. 'Three cases for Matthew Lovelace, one for Martha Lovelace, your wife and – one each for your children, Justice Lovelace and Prudence Lovelace. They were sent aboard, sir – about half an hour ago. Six cases altogether.'

6

'Thank you,' said Mr Lovelace. 'At what time do we set sail?'

'We sail on the afternoon tide, sir. About three in the afternoon.'

'At what time can we go aboard?'

'We shall be taking on the passengers, sir, about noon.'

'Very well, we shall be here in good time,' he said. With that, he turned his back on the sailor. The four of them, Matthew, Martha and their two children, Justice and Prudence picked their way through the crowd. Almost at once, they disappeared in the surging multitude. Like the very sea itself, the lingering mass of humanity surged back and the Lovelaces could be seen no more.

2 Going Aboard

It was a quarter to mid-day. Matthew Lovelace and his wife and children were once again back upon the waterfront, but this time they were not the only Pilgrims. There were many other families dressed just as they. Men with wide-brimmed, tall black hats and their wives in white. The Pilgrims were gathering to go aboard the *Speedwell* and the *Mayflower*. A strident voice rang out 'Prepare to embark. Prepare to embark.'

With that the Pilgrims moved slowly forward and gathered at the head of the steps that led down to the rowing boats below. At a signal from one of the Pilgrims, the men took off their hats and bowed their heads. The children stopped their wild excitement and a deadly hush came over all the waterfront. Everything fell still and silent, apart from the occasional bark of a stray dog. The lapping of the water could be distinctly heard. The silence could be felt. Suddenly a man's voice broke the spell. One of the Pilgrims began to speak. He began to pray in a deep and solemn voice. As he proceeded his voice grew louder. He could be heard all over the waterfront. He asked that God would have his hand upon them and bless them in their coming journey; that he would prosper them, protect them and land them safe in America. All the Pilgrims were united in their prayers. Subdued throaty amen-murmurs could be heard as the man proceeded. As the Pilgrim came to the end of his prayer, he offered up thanks to God for his blessing upon their lives up to then. Then he sounded his final 'Amen'. The whole company of the Pilgrims added their voices to his and a great swelling 'Amen' sounded across the water and reached far out, even to the ships in the bay.

The men then donned their hats. Tears were in many eyes. Silence reigned once more. The company shuffled steadily forward to the head of the steps. The Pilgrims began to descend in orderly company into the rowing boats, men, women and children. The Pilgrims were leaving.

The rowing boats were quickly filled with their excited human cargo. But the excitement was subdued. The heavy felt silence still dominated the whole scene. Some orders rang out. A boat was filled and the sailors pulled with the oars. Soon the bay was dotted with little bobbing boats making their way towards the two sea-going vessels.

Within a matter of minutes the Lovelaces came alongside. The sailors held the frisking boat tight against the vessel which towered above them. Matthew, Martha and their two children began to climb aboard the *Speedwell*, clambering and pulling hand over fist at the twisting rope ladder as it dangled over its edge. They breasted the side of the ship. A forest of hands heaved them over. In no time at all, the four of them were standing, albeit somewhat shaken and dishevelled, upon the deck of the tiny ship. They straightened themselves, smoothing their ruffled clothes. Mrs Lovelace fussed hen-like about her chicks.

'So – this is the *Speedwell*,' said Mr Lovelace, looking about him. He slowly shook his head. He tried to impart a cheery note to his words.

Indeed it was. This was the cockleshell they hoped would land them safely in Virginia.

'Father,' said Justice looking up to him, his eyes and voice betraying his eagerness, 'May I and Prudence go and explore the ship?'

'Yes – yes, you may, my son,' replied his father with a smile. 'But, you must be careful. Don't get into any mischief. Leave things alone that do not belong to you.'

'Yes, Father, I promise. Come on,' called Justice to his sister, Prudence – tugging feverishly at her dress and already moving away. 'Come on. Let's go and see what we can find.'

The deck upon which they stood was very tiny. All around, were coils of rope, spars and rolled-up sails and boxes of a most interesting and inviting nature. The children looked about them, drinking in their new world, eyes and mouths wide open. Sailors brushed by them speaking their seemingly foreign tongue. They were a motley crew. They wore such a variety of garb. Shirts of every hue, faded jackets and hats of every description and some that defied all description. Ragged trousers, rudely torn off at the knee. Patches and stripes in profusion. The children thought that every colour that ever was, must be featured in the sailors' clothes.

At one end of the deck there was an inviting black hole with steps steeply descending below. The steps quickly disappeared in a way that aroused much curiosity.

'Come on,' said Justice, 'let's go down below and see what we can find. Where do these steps lead, I wonder?'

They scrambled down the narrow, well-worn steps and immediately were lost in complete blackness. It hit them like a wall. It stopped them in their tracks. It almost took their breath away. No, 'twas not complete blackness. Pale pools of dirty yellow light were cast here and there by spluttering tallow candles held in tarnished brass lanterns around the sides of the vessel. For a moment or two the children could see nothing – but – then – their eyes gradually grew accustomed to the dim sallow light that was shed upon the scene by the bleary flares. They could begin to make out vague shadows and strange shapes cast by the weak, flickering lights.

They saw the place was crowded with Pilgrim families, just like their own, who were trying to make space for themselves in the corners, nooks and crannies of this tiny vessel. Some were spreading blankets upon the floor and placing bundles for stop-gap pillows for weary heads. Boxes grated across the

10

harsh wooden floor as they resisted the efforts to arrange them as makeshift rough furniture.

So – this was to be their home for the next two or three months! This would take them across the ocean to America.

'Where's the beds?' queried Prudence. 'Will we have no bed to sleep upon?' said she to her brother.

Justice took a manly stance and air. With legs apart and hands upon his hips, he made his reply. 'No, of course not, silly. We have so little space. We shall be crammed together all the way across the ocean. We shall have to lie upon the floor, I expect.'

They turned their eyes from the scene. They preferred to forget the hard wooden bed to come – and the cramped space.

'Let's go down to the next deck.' Justice had had his curiosity aroused and it demanded further satisfaction.

'Yes, let's,' agreed his sister – she being no sluggard to find further wonders.

They gingerly picked their way across the deck past the boxes, around the people – who hardly noticed them – so engrossed were they in setting up their new homes. The children carefully groped their way down the dark, unguarded steps to the black hold below.

The same scene as before was repeated before their eyes. The place was alive with Pilgrim families who were staking out their possession of the precious tiny deck space. The gloom was full of strange shadows, dancing wildly in the faltering light, flickering and jumping on the walls. Boxes stood all round. The children yielded to their itching fingers. In no time, they were lifting lids of inviting boxes, peering and poking into crevices, their eyes and mouths growing wider and wider with wonder.

As they stood there drinking it all in, a sailor pushed his way roughly past them. 'Make way there, you young'uns. Keep out of my way, will'ee?'

'Please sir, what's down below?' said Justice, tugging at the man's shirt before he disappeared into the gloom.

'Down below, laddie? Why, it's the stores down there. All the food we are going to eat. All the tools we're goin'aneed. All the water we'll drink – that's what's down there. An' 'tis no place for the likes of you. We don't want any children down there, so you stay above the stores. D'you hear me?'

He grabbed the children and roughly pulled them towards him. He bared his teeth. They shone white – well, nearly white – in the murky light. 'You never know what might happen to littl'uns – down there.' He put his head back and guffawed. The laugh seemed to pierce the children's ears and reach right to the pit of their stomachs. He pushed his face into theirs. He was not laughing now. 'You stay on this deck and above. Go on now. Off with you. D'you hear me? You stay above the stores.'

With that he released his grip, pushed the children away and was gone. The children shook with fear.

'Let's find Mother and Father again,' said Prudence to her brother, her mouth dry. 'Let's see what space we've got to live in.'

'Yes – let's – that's a good idea,' said Justice in reply. He swallowed, deeply. He was relieved to hear Prudence change the subject. He hoped she had not heard the fear in his trembling dry voice nor felt it in his shaking hand.

They climbed the steps, manoeuvred their way across the hold and up the steps again and so out on to the open deck. They had to shut their eyes against the blazing of the sun as they came out from the dimness below. They had not realized how bright was the day above, nor how dark the night below. However, their eyes quickly grew accustomed to the glare and soon they noticed their mother standing across the deck, anxiously looking for them.

'Here we are, Mother,' they cried out.

'And there *you* are', she replied, with obvious relief. 'Where *have* you been?' She did not wait for an answer. 'Come on, you two, and see the place we've found to live.'

They reached out their hands to grip their mother's outstretched welcome. Together they made their way to another hatchway, descended again into the hold below and soon were united with their father. Their few boxes had been placed about to try to give them a measure of privacy. They tried to make themselves as snug as uninviting boards would allow. In next to no time, they were seated upon the floor with their backs pressed against the wooden sides of the vessel.

Their father spoke to them, wagging his finger at them to give added emphasis. 'Now, my children, this is all the space we shall have for the next few weeks.' He tapped the few boxes around them. 'You must mark carefully where we live. You must not get lost. You must keep your few possessions in careful order and you must not stray into the space of others. Remember we shall live and sleep here for many weeks. This is our home until we reach America.'

Mrs Lovelace added her counsel. 'You can see how cramped the hold is,' she said. 'There is very little light – even with the hatches open you can hardly see a hand in front of your face. But what is more worrying is that there is so little air. We must spend as much time as we can on the open deck. That is what we must do. When the storms come, we shall be compelled to stay below – maybe for days at a time. So get above whenever you can.'

This ominous prediction of stifling days below, filled the children with much fear. They looked about them. It was hard to see things clearly in the near pitch blackness below. But they made out others just like themselves. Families huddled together. They heard the whimpering of bewildered children. Others were separated from their parents and frantically calling out. Some people had the wrong boxes. One chest had been dropped and all its precious contents spilled across the floor. All seemed chaos and confusion. The blackness could almost be felt. The rancid smell of tallow dips filled the air.

'Are you afraid?' said Prudence, lifting her head quietly to her father.

He looked down, a gentle smile upon his lips. 'No, my child, no, my child', came the solemn, but reassuring reply. 'God will be with us. God will keep us.'

3 Casting off

A T three o'clock, the Lovelace family was on open deck once again. They stood in company with many other similar families at the side of the ship, looking back with saddened eyes towards the shore. All around them sailors were clambering cat-like up the rigging, pulling at the sheets.

It seemed in no time at all that the great sails were unfurled. Above the din, they heard the sound of the captain's orders. The shouts ran along the deck. They heard the resisting ropes squeal as the anchor was pulled from the sea up on to the ship. It resented the disturbance of its slumbers and it spued the splashing waters all over the deck in protest. They felt the wind take up the enormous expanse of canvas with a heave and the beams and spars creaked in rebellion. The ship seemed to sense the weeks of weary labour ahead. She started to move. She was under way! The Pilgrims felt her shudder. She groaned as she left her calm place of rest. She shook herself and resisted the unwarranted intrusion into her peace. The open sea certainly did not beckon her. She had seen and felt too much of the wide ocean before. It possessed no charms. She knew what was waiting to greet her only too well.

Ahead of them, the Pilgrims observed their sister ship, the *Mayflower*, already getting up speed. They noticed the great waves of the sea churning and creaming into white froth at her bows. Then they felt their own ship heave and lurch. She pulled over with the force of the wind. They had to grip the side to keep themselves upright. They heard the rush of the water as she began to cut through the waves. They were off! The open sea was before them.

They were moving! They had said 'goodbye' to England. America was ahead. America! They took their last longing look back to the shore. They could hear the cheering of the crowd lining the quay. Good wishes raced across the water to reach them: 'God bless you', 'God bless you'. They picked out black-cloaked men upon the cobbles as they waved them fond 'goodbyes'.

The Lovelaces felt that with God with them in the ship and such praying friends behind on the shore, they were able to look forward with confidence. They turned away from the shore and looked out to the sea. They scanned the horizon. 'What unknown dangers await us there? . . . What

16

will the voyage be like? . . . What will life be like in that cramped hold below? . . . Will we meet storms? . . . Indeed, will we ever step on to dry land again?'

4 *First Morning at Sea*

IT was very early the next morning. Justice was curled up on the boarded floor of the dark confined hold in that happy, hazy, half-world between sleep and wakefulness. He was dimly aware that his back ached and his legs were stiff. He felt so sore, lying there on the hard wooden deck. The blanket that covered him was rough and coarse. His head was pressed against the hard calico bundle that served as his pillow. It smelt so strange and it prickled his face. He was dimly conscious of the rise and fall of the ship with its gentle lurch against the waves. He could just make out the subdued murmurs about him – the contented grunts and snorings – mothers consoling their whimpering babies – a snapping dog – the unfamiliar rattles of a sea-going vessel – the whistlings, murmurings and groanings of sleeping men who were having their elbows knocked and their legs trod upon. The hazy noises mingled together. He gave up the struggle to sort them all out . . . Does Prudence feel like this, he wondered? He lifted his head. Tallow smoke filled the air. Shadows danced and flickered in the eerie, yellow, half-light cast by the spluttering candle wicks. He saw his father, already awake, sitting up, with his hatless head bowed over the great, fat leather book in his hand. The pages were yellow, cracked and stained by a thousand thumbmarks. He was holding a candle close to the page. He was reading intently. His eyes were fixed upon the words before him – he pored over the book. Just beyond his father, Justice could make out Prudence as she lay close to her mother, both of them still gently sleeping. He

18

saw their bodies rising and gently falling back as they breathed
– blissfully unaware of their bitter surroundings.

Justice rubbed his eyes. 'You're awake then, my boy,' said
Mr Lovelace – his voice breaking into his son's thoughts. 'Feel
a bit stiff, eh?' A smile crept to his lips at the sight of his son
rubbing his legs and arms.

Justice stirred himself and yawned. He stretched himself
but immediately wished he hadn't; his hand had clouted
against a hard, a very hard and unforgiving oak buttress and
his head had slipped off the pillow to the wooden floor. He
had thought the pillow hard enough but now he knew better.
Now he remembered . . . he wasn't in his bed at home . . .
He was at sea . . . He was on the *Speedwell* bound for America.
He lay still and began to drop back into the mixed world of
dream and daydream. He could just pick out the low beams
above him. 'How much has happened over the past few
months,' he thought. 'We've not had a settled home and –
more important to me – a settled bed for weeks. All those
weary walks in Holland! My legs ache even now at the
thought . . . The voyage across the sea to England and all the
upheavals we had there . . . and now . . . this hard cramped
hold which has to be our home for the coming months as we
sail over this wild and unknown ocean . . . home! . . .
Why? . . . Why? . . .' He could hear the unaccustomed noises
that would prove to be his companions over many weeks. A
strange, hissing, sucking of water as it squealed through the
bilges. The gentle singing of the sea and the sighing of the
ship in reply.

'What time is it, Father?' he asked sleepily.

'Just past five,' came the whispered reply.

Justice drifted back into his dreams. 'Will it be a fine day?'
he mused . . . 'Will there be any storms today? . . . I wonder . . .? I wonder . . .? How fast are we going? . . . What
will we do today . . .? What will we have for food . . .?'

As if his father had heard his thoughts, his deep voice broke in upon his son's daydreams. 'Your mother is waking up. We shall soon break our fast.'

Within a few minutes, the four of them were all awake and sitting up. They hunched themselves together, drew close with their backs pressed against the pitiless boards. Before them they had laid their simple breakfast. Simple was the word! It had not taken much preparation. The children felt that there was nothing very exciting about it. A clean white

napkin had been placed on the floor. Their food was laid in three small heaps upon the sheet. It consisted of a pile of dry biscuits, some pieces of salt beef and a few green apples. Leastways, that's how it appeared to the children. Things were very difficult to sort out in the murky darkness. Before they began to eat, Mr Lovelace gave thanks to God for the provision of the food. Then they started to eat the dry biscuits. Justice reached out and picked up one. He broke it into small pieces. It snapped in his hands and he felt how hard it was. But that was not the worst. Oh! how terrible they tasted! He thought they felt so hard in his hands but they were far worse in his mouth.

And so dry. They took an age to chew and swallow. He could not get them down.

'And this is all we shall have,' he thought, 'all the time we are aboard.' But he would not voice his thoughts. He could not. He dare not. Had they not just thanked God for his provision? Had his father not often told him they had to undergo such hardships if they were ever to reach the land of freedom? And he knew that his father was right. It was far better to serve God even if that meant a life of hardship for them now. He knew that, whatever the cost, they must live for God and not live in ease, and serve themselves.

The salt beef, in its turn, lived up to its name too. It *was* salty. Very! Both the children pulled grimaces as they ate. They screwed their faces at the hard, bitter food. The apples proved little better. They too were hard and very sour.

'Cheer up, my dears,' consoled their mother. She had noticed their looks of anguish at the bitter food. 'We shall get used to it and it's only for a while.'

After breakfast, Mr Lovelace opened his big leather Bible. The Lovelace family, like all the Pilgrims, always began each day with Bible reading and prayer. They would not change their habits just because they were at sea. He read some verses to the family – very slowly. Then he bowed his hatless head and prayed for God's blessing upon the family in the day before them. The mother and the children bowed their heads with Mr Lovelace. He prayed for protection on the voyage. He prayed that God would use them in their lives for his glory. He made mention of each of the family in particular. He spoke of the special dangers and temptations that might befall them. He closed in thanks to God for his mercy and goodness to them.

At the end of family prayers, there was a short time of silence. Then Mr Lovelace slapped his thigh and put his long arms about them all.

'Let's all take a walk on deck, shall we?'

They were so cramped in their quarters below and the air

was so stifling that they needed all the fresh air they could get. Mrs Lovelace quickly folded the napkin and carefully placed it back amongst her possessions. They all tidied their rough bedding. They pulled themselves to their feet. Mr Lovelace rose and tried to stand upright. But, before he could straighten his back, his head hit the beams of the low ceiling of the deck above. He put his hand quickly to his brow. The children heard him suck in air with the pain.

'Are you all right, my love?' came the anxious cry of his wife.

'Yes, my dear – thank you. 'Twill keep me humble – this low roof,' he said with a wry smile upon his face. 'I shall not be able to hold my head erect down here, that's for sure. Come, my dears,' he turned to the children. 'Come, let's go up. Let's get some real air – and let me stand up straight.'

They picked their way carefully to the foot of the stairs and soon they were standing upon the deck in the dim dawn light. What surprised Justice was that he could see nothing but sea. There was no land in sight at all. Then he began to make out a dim, grey smudge on the horizon as his eyes grew accustomed to the feeble light.

'That's England,' said his father, anticipating the unasked question.

'England?' cried Prudence.

'Yes, my dears – we are out so far that that is all you can see of that great land of ours.'

They were heading into the West, the morning sun rising behind them. Far out in the West, they could see dark black clouds on the horizon. Above them, they heard the wind beating furiously into the sails. The canvas snapped in reply. They felt the ship rising and falling on the waves. They saw the white horses riding the ocean around them. Justice felt the wind tugging at his hair. He sensed his father's strong arm upon his shoulder.

'We'll have a storm come up today, my son. We shall not

have to wait long to get our sea legs. The ocean will introduce us very quickly to its power. Look out there,' he went on, raising his arm to the West, 'we're heading for a storm all right.'

The wind was already rising and the first drops of spume began to beat upon the ship. The spray hit them in the face. They bent their heads. Justice felt the sting of the salt in his eyes and – as he licked his lips – he tasted its tang. He lifted his face and looked out to the West once again. His eyes gave away his inward fear. The sky merged into the distant sea. The yellow sun, from behind, played upon the greyness of cloud and water before them.

He heard the ship groan and creak with the force of the wind above her and the power of the sea beneath. The Lovelaces stood on deck, facing into the wind. They stood there for a long time. No one said a word. Father and mother stood with the children between them. The wind continued to scream about them. It increased its force and power. The wind blew droplets of spray into their faces. The *Speedwell* began to climb higher in the waves and then she fell down – down, down into the depths of the sea. Justice felt his stomach moving in sympathy (rather, out of sympathy) with her. He felt queezy. He wished he'd not eaten his breakfast . . .

Suddenly, the bows hit into the waves and a great surge of white-topped water came across the prow and on to the deck, swilling against them and drenching them in the legs. The sea was slapping against the side of the vessel, laughingly calling her to play. The wind joined in the chorus. It whipped the yards. It began to yell in the rigging and smack against the sails. It screamed for attention.

'I think it's time we went below,' said Mr Lovelace to the family. He had to cup his hands to his mouth and shout because of the screech of the wind in the rigging.

Just as he spoke, another great surge of water crossed on to the ship and pounded the boards. The *Speedwell* lurched. She staggered. She seemed to drop into nothingness. Then she was on her wallowing way once again. The beams creaked and groaned even more. The sails smacked and snarled angrily in the wind. The waves began to beat upon the deck and the wind and the spray whipped into their faces. The elements no longer called for the ship to play. As though the *Speedwell* had declined the offer and thus offended the sea and wind, they now combined to try to destroy her.

The Lovelaces made their way, as best they could, across the swilling deck towards the hatch that led below. As they began to scramble down the stairway another great wall of grey-green water came across the deck. It drenched them this time completely and to the skin. The water chased them down the stairs hitting, smacking, pulling and pushing, carrying all before it.

In between decks, chaos reigned. Salt water was everywhere. It slopped from side to side, chasing across the hold.

'Batten down the hatches,' came the raucous cry. 'Quick! Quick man, batten down the hatches.'

The hatches were pulled over, slammed shut and lashed tight with ropes. At once all was darkness below the hatches. In the dim light cast by the tallows, Justice and Prudence looked on the reigning confusion. Pots and pans and bundles had been scattered anyhow by the force of the water. Precious belongings had been flung in every direction. Chaos was king. The hold was full of drenched and tumbling humanity. Arms and legs stuck out everywhere at the oddest angles. Everything was wet through. Saturated blankets and pillows were strewn about all over the place. It was a babel of noise. All was topsy-turvy. Children, everywhere, were crying. One young girl had a horrible gash across her forehead and a swelling red bruise where she had been hurled against a beam. Men and women were furiously scrabbling in corners, desperately pulling and tugging in vain attempts to recover their few possessions. Everyone was shouting.

The ship continued to lurch from one side to the other,

rolling and pitching in the force of the wind and waves. The hold seemed to be one thick porridge of people and property swilling about in sea water. The world had taken leave of its senses. It had gone mad.

5 Sorrow Down Below

Mr Lovelace grabbed at – and held on to – a beam. Justice clutched his arms around his father's leg and held on for very life. Mrs Lovelace clung to the steps that led above, her knuckles white under the strain. Prudence gripped her mother's skirt. She buried her face deep in the folds of her apron. She desperately wished to hide from the hideous chaos.

'Order! please,' rang out the strong voice of Mr Lovelace. 'Order! please!'

He had a dreadful task to make his lone voice heard above the scream of the wind, the shouts of the people and the relentless battering of the waves. But, gradually, the human noise died down and all that was left was the raging of the elements outside. The people began to pick themselves up. They held their heads bent, forced down by the lowness of the beams but also by the confusion of their shame.

'This is no way to face the storm,' said Mr Lovelace sternly. 'Do we trust in God? Let's show our trust to the ungodly that are with us on this voyage. What a dreadful testimony we are to God's goodness – behaving like this! It's our first storm – we shall have many more – and look at us!' He waved an arm.

The people listened with their heads bowed and their eyes cast to their feet. As they listened, they grew more and more ashamed at their lack of self-discipline in the face of trouble.

Mr Lovelace went on to give orders to the company. There was a softer pitch to his voice. 'Get yourselves sorted out. Come, my friends. Get your things,' he said. 'Get them back to your quarters. Let's settle down again. Move, I say. Move, there!'

Within a few minutes, something like order had been restored. Chaos yielded to order once again. The pots and pans had all been rescued. Precious, cherished bundles were restored to their rightful place once more. All movable objects had been lashed securely with ropes. Once again, families were settled in their little groups. Wounds were being tenderly bound and bandaged. Discipline reigned below once again.

But all was chaos outside. The ship continued to lurch violently. The winds still roared about her mercilessly. The waves were, by now, crashing right on to the main deck above. But down below, the people, although in almost total darkness and cramped and sore, were mainly protected from the worst of the tempest.

Prudence sat with the small of her back pressed against the hard boards of the ship. She was lashed, like her parents and brother by strong cords about her waist. These kept her right against the side of the ship. Her mother's arm was tight about her too. This gave her consolation and comfort. Prudence felt cold. She was soaked to the skin by the sea-water. She shivered. She felt like crying but she bravely fought back her tears. She knew she must not cry . . . She bit her lip. She could taste the salt . . . She could restrain herself no longer. She felt the warm trickle of the tear down her face. She tasted its saltiness . . . She was beginning to cry in silence. She bent her head. She tried to hide her face. She felt afraid and ashamed.

'I must not cry. I must not,' she repeated to herself. She drummed the words into her mind. She pressed her fingers deep into her palms. But she was unable to hold back the salty stream. Her tears flooded down her face. Her chest heaved with deep sobs.

Her mother's arm clutched her even more tightly. 'Do not be afraid, my child,' she said. 'God will not leave us. Do not

be afraid. "His way is in the whirlwind and the storm, and
clouds are the dust of his feet. He rebukes the sea and dries it
up . . . The LORD is good, a refuge in times of trouble. He
cares for those who trust in him . . ." ' Her mother's voice
sounded so sure and steady.

'Will we die, Mother? Will this tiny ship of ours be able
to overcome these waves? Will we be smashed against the
rocks?'

As she spoke the ship gave another mighty lurch. Prudence's
face peered up anxiously at her mother. She was just able to
make out her tender smile. She looked so serene. Her mother
bent her head down toward her. Prudence felt her mother's
warm soft cheek gently pressed against her brow. Her mother
kissed her and pressed her close.

'No, my child. No . . . God cares for those who trust in
him.'

'How do you know that, Mother?' Prudence listened to her

28

wavering trembling voice. She was unable to hide her fear.
'How do you know we shall be safe? How do you know?'

'God has told us so, my child. He told us long ago through
his prophet Nahum in the Old Testament. And God never
breaks his Word. Never! He will bring us through – you'll
see.'

The two fell silent. Mrs Lovelace placed her head back
against the side of the ship. She closed her eyes. Prudence
sensed her tears drying. She closed her eyes and clutched her
mother closely. She pressed her face into her mother's dress.
Softly, so softly Mrs Lovelace began to sing, her eyes still
gently closed. Prudence gladly drank in the words. How
sweet they were! They came from the book of the Psalms –
the forty-sixth.

'God is our refuge and strength, an ever present help in
trouble. Therefore we will not fear though the earth give way
and the mountains fall into the heart of the sea, though its
waters roar and foam and the mountains quake with their
surging.'

Mrs Lovelace's soft voice wavered not. The family next to
them caught the song. It spread like wild-fire around the hold
and soon the whole company was joined in the swelling
chorus. It reached above the violence of the raging of the
storm outside. The Pilgrims all sang together, 'Be still, and
know that I am God . . . The LORD Almighty is with us;
The God of Jacob is our fortress.'

The sea and wind made their own roaring contribution,
but the mounting tide of the Pilgrims' song overcame the
tumult of the elements.

Mrs Lovelace glanced down. Prudence had fallen into a
gentle sleep with a soft smile upon her lips. Mrs Lovelace
held her close. She closed her own eyes and leant her head
back upon the hard beam behind her. She sighed, softly.
'How good,' she thought, 'how good it is to have the Lord of
the ocean – the Lord God Almighty with us in this tiny ship.'

6 *We're Leaking!*

THE long, long morning passed slowly, dragging its weary feet. The two children fitfully slept whilst the ship ploughed her punishing way through the storm. In common with nearly all the Pilgrims, the children were seasick. The awful nausea continued by the hour. The longed-for relief seemed to get further away than ever. 'Will it never come? Will it never come?'

Eventually, Justice sat up. He pulled his knees up to his chest and hunched himself together with his arms clasped about his legs. After a while, he pressed his aching head back against the side of the ship and stretched his arms and hands upwards and backwards. He was startled to find he could feel water trickling down the side of the vessel. He turned his head, knitting his brow. He madly scraped his fingers along the boards and although he could not clearly see, he could – just – pick out the place where sea-water was breaching the boards.

'We're leaking, Father,' he gasped, shaking his father's arm. 'We're leaking! Father, feel this.' Justice grabbed his father's hand and drew it to the place where he had found the water. 'The ship is leaking.'

Mr Lovelace hastily traced his fingers along the crack that Justice had found. He peered into the gloom. 'Fetch me a lantern,' he said quickly and quietly. 'Make haste.' He spent a few silent moments carefully examining the boards. 'You're right, my son,' he exclaimed with a faint whistle as he held the flickering light close. 'You're right. The boards are being

pulled apart by the force of the wind and the sea.' He stopped.
His fingers came to his chin and gently caressed it. 'I overheard
some such talk on the quay. Some gossiping old sailors were
talking, I remember. They said they thought this vessel would
leak because she carried too much sail for her size. I didn't
believe it at the time but I see it's true.' He looked around at
his wife. 'Something must be done about it. Something must
be done,' he said through his teeth.

'Are you sure, my dear?' said Mrs Lovelace. She placed her
hand upon her husband's. 'Are you sure? Surely they would
not put us out to sea in such a state. No!' She shook her head.
' 'Tis only wild talk you have heard. Surely it will be all
right?' But her voice gave away her lack of confidence.

'No, my dear, I fear not.' There was no smile upon his face
as he spoke. 'No! something must be done.' His mind was
made up. He quickly undid the knots, wrestling with the
cord about his waist. 'Oh, my cold wet fingers!' he said, as
the rope slipped in his grasp. But soon, with his pulling and

31

tugging, the knot yielded. He slid himself along to the next man, pulling himself along by means of the many boxes stacked around. He bent his head towards the man. Justice barely heard their murmured conversation mingled with the many other voices of the hold. He saw the man put his hand up along the side of the vessel. The man turned to face Mr Lovelace. Justice discerned the alarm in his eyes, by the light of the lantern – feeble though it was. He caught his gasp and managed to get hold of his words. 'You're right, Matthew. She is leaking.'

Their heads bent together and Justice lost the remaining words of the conversation. After a moment or two Mr Lovelace crawled back to his place once again and tied himself in. 'We shall have to wait until the storm dies down,' said he, anticipating the question that his wife needed not to ask. 'As soon as we can, we shall get a small number of us together to go and face the Master of the vessel. It's no use going on with the ship in this dreadful state. We cannot try to cross the Atlantic Ocean in such an unseaworthy vessel as this. It would be the height of madness. Let's hope the storm soon blows itself out. I don't fancy many more hours of this with only leaking boards to protect us.' His voice had fallen to a mere whisper. He beckoned his family close. 'Listen,' he confided. 'Please do not sound an alarm. There's nothing we can do at this height of the storm. Do not alarm the rest. Wait patiently. We shall have the matter put right at the first opportunity.'

7 Exploring

A COUPLE more weary, dragging hours passed and the storm, though still raging, began to abate. Prudence leaned across her mother and father who, by now had drifted into a shallow, jerky sleep. She tugged at her brother's tunic. 'Are you awake?' she whispered.

'Ssh,' hissed Justice, in reply. 'You'll awaken Father.'

'I've had enough of sitting here, haven't you? Do you feel like exploring?' she said.

Justice needed no second invitation. They cast rapid, furtive glances about them. Their parents were asleep. Their neighbours were asleep. Now was the time. Now! Quickly they slipped their ropes, the knots submitting to their eager fingers. They were free. Prudence pulled Justice close. She whispered in his ear. 'Down below.' She motioned towards the steps.

They scuttled as fast as they could to the steps that led below. In no time at all they had slipped down to the lower deck.

'Let's go down to the stores and see what damage the sea-water has done.' Prudence had a mischievous glint in her eyes.

'You know we were forbidden to go down there. Remember – by that horrible sailor,' said Justice in a voice that tended to falter slightly.

Prudence could detect that he would not long resist. 'You're afraid,' she said.

'No – I'm not – not really afraid.'

33

'Well, if you won't come with me, I shall go alone,' she said defiantly. With that she was gone.

Justice hesitated. But only for a moment. He was being tugged both ways at once. He felt his qualms holding him back like a chain – but his curiosity pulled him down, much as a magnet draws a nail. He shrugged his shoulders as one who had made his decision, cast caution to the wind and he too disappeared into the gaping hole. He immediately missed his footing and fell down the first few steps. He was only stopped from hurtling all the way to the bottom by crashing into his sister.

'Ssh!' she hissed. 'Ssh! you'll have us caught. Can't you mind where you are going?'

'Sorry.' Justice was much abashed. 'I slipped.' They stopped and listened. It was all right. They had not been discovered. They could hear nothing but the hissing of the sea. No! That was not all. They could just – only just – detect the sound of human voices. Faraway voices. But the sound came not from above. It beckoned from below. They could not sort out the words of the conversation – the voices were too distant and indistinct for that. But both children had a longing to find out more. An insatiable longing. They could see nothing at all below. Justice inched his way down the steps as carefully as he could. The voices grew louder and more distinct. Still he could see nothing. His sister kept close behind. Gradually a veiled dimness of light came into view. A large beam, just at head height, loomed before Justice. He ducked his head below the offending joist. He saw the stores hold spread out before him. The light and conversation came from a far corner. There, a huddle of sailors had a rough sea-chest decked as a table with a bottle and glasses upon it. Justice saw it all in the light cast by a tallow dip upon the table. Coins glinted in the flickering light.

The sailors did not look up to notice their observer. Their attention was solidly fixed upon the pressing business of the gambling table before them. Justice withdrew his head from

34

the hole. He put his mouth close to his sister's ear. 'Men – sailors – gambling,' he whispered. He gently pulled her sleeve. 'Come on.'

8 *A Plot Discovered*

'COME on,' said Justice.
'No,' replied Prudence. Her bravery had vanished.
'No. I'm frightened.'

'Come on,' said Justice. 'Let's go down and see what they are doing.'

Prudence felt too frightened to stay alone in the dark. She had to go on with her brother. They slid like silent snakes down the remaining steps. Soon they were knee-deep in spades and axes. Carefully they picked their way across the hold, through the tools, over the sacks and past the boxes. Once, Justice stepped on to a pile of tools and lost his balance with the moving of the ship in the heavy sea. He dislodged a pile of muskets and they fell with a clatter down amongst the chests. Justice froze – froze with horror. Prudence grabbed him and pulled him down to the safety of the darkness. She put her finger to her clenched lips. They could feel and hear their hearts pounding madly within them.

'What's that?' demanded a thick drunken voice. The question was repeated, louder. 'What's that, I say.' One of the sailors stood up. He picked up the tallow dip and held it high above his head. 'What's that noise? Who's there?'

Justice and Prudence froze – stiff with fear. They dared not move. They shrank back against the boxes.

'Come on, Nabal, sit down, will you?' called a befuddled voice from the gambling party. 'Put that light back down here. 'Tis only the sea pulled over some muskets.'

'Aye,' said another, 'aye, or maybe some rats. Come on,

36

man, it's your throw. Sit down, Nabal, and get on with the game.'

'No! I will not. There's somebody there, I tell you. Somebody's a-spy'n on us.'

Justice and Prudence could see him, as they peered around some sacks. His eyes were filled with fear, rapidly searching the piles of sacks and chests.

'Sit down, man. Get on with the game.'

Justice and Prudence heard a scuffle. The thought that the drunken sailor was coming over towards them raced through their minds. But no! Relief! It was merely the sound of the rest of his friends pulling their gaming partner back.

' 'Tis your turn,' a drunken voice drawled out. ' 'Tis your turn. Noise! Noise! Forget the noise. 'Tis only rats. Get on with the important business.'

Justice and Prudence started to breathe again as the subdued sounds of the resumed game reached them. All had grown a concealing dark once more. After a few moments, Justice began to inch his way towards the men. Prudence wanted to go back, but she dared not leave her brother. After what seemed an age, they managed to get very close to the sailors who were once again engrossed in their game. The children hid behind sacks of dried peas where they could see and hear all before them.

Suddenly, the game was over. With oaths and curses, three of the men abruptly threw down their money, leaving the fourth to pick up the scattered coins.

'Another?' he said, a cheerful ring of anticipation in his voice, 'another game?'

'No fear,' replied one of his companions. 'I have nothing left as 'tis. Do you want the very shirt off my back, too?'

'Well, let's have another noggin afore we go.'

'Aye, another noggin.'

Glasses were filled with fiery liquid. Four heads were flung back and the spirits rapidly disappeared down gaping throats. The men talked on in their tipsy way. As they spoke the children felt a tingle of horror run through them. The sailors were laughing and joking about – about them! Them!

'Ah! ah! That's good that is. They Pilgrims have been deceived – deceived good and proper,' bragged one as he took another swig at the bottle. He wiped his mouth with his sleeve, or what remained of his ragged shirt upon his arm.

He passed the bottle to his friend. He, too, thrust the bottle to his lips and tipped his arm and took a long guzzling drink. He was so flushed and shaky that the liquid poured over his chin and spilled down his shirt. He belched loudly. He slapped the bottle unsteadily on to the table. 'Ah,' said he. 'Ah, good and proper, they've been had.' He laughed loudly. 'Master Reynolds is a clever one. He's taken them in all right,' he sneered.

'What's all this? What's all this? What's his plan, then,' questioned another.

'What, don't you know?' came the reply. 'Reynolds has a great scheme. He's a sly boots, he is. He's right cunning, you've got to hand it to him all right. He's a sharp one and no mistake. I all'us said he was crafty.'

'Yes, yes. We know that! But what's he done,' came the

impatient demand. 'What's so clever? What's he up to this time?'

'All right! All right! Keep your temper. It's like this. He plans to get this lot,' he jerked his thumb upwards – 'he's goin' to get this lot well out into the Atlantic and by then she'll be leaking good and proper. Ah, good and proper! Then, he'll turn her back – the Pilgrims will beg him like as not – and then he'll be able to dump them back on shore – and at their asking.' He guffawed, took another swig at the bottle and went on. ' 'Tis like this. The plan is, he'll have made his money for crossing the Atlantic by just going out for a few days. See? And there again, even if they do make him go all the way, he'll bring the ship back after she's unloaded. They think that he's staying with them a full year – and what's more they've paid their money. They've paid it already. Think of that! Paid already! He's a clever one, that Master Reynolds. That he is. I all'us said he was artful.'

'Silence, you fools. Silence!'

In an instant all eyes were turned to the steps. So engrossed had been the sailors and the children – so absorbed – no one had noticed the descent of another man down the steps. A massive man now stood at the foot of the steps, one hand clutching the beam and a lantern held high in the other. He wore a magnificent tunic of bright blue with gold buttons. How they shone in the light of his lantern! His long hair fell about his collar. He had a frilly white cravat tucked beneath his chin that rode magnificently over his chest. A thick, glossy black leather belt crossed from his shoulder to his waist. It was Master Reynolds himself, the captain of the ship. Master Reynolds!

'Silence.' The captain slowly walked towards the men. He picked his way, faultlessly, through the maze of sacks and chests. 'You fools. You besotted fools,' he shouted at them. 'I'll have you keel-hauled for this. Keel-hauled, d'you hear me?' he roared. 'I'll have you flogged at the main mast. You'll feel the cat o' nine tails. Disobedience to my orders, I will not tolerate. "No drink down here," I said. Did I not say that? Did I not say that?'

But no reply was forthcoming.

He reached the men. 'What's this? What's this?' he said, picking up a stray coin. 'Gaming eh? You know my orders, Nabal Wilson,' he said pointing his finger at the chest of one and prodding him. 'You know my orders, man. And my orders are to be obeyed! I'll have you keel-hauled, you lazy swab.' He fell silent. He looked at the shame-faced sailors who had, by now, rapidly sobered up.

He put a brown-booted foot upon the table and slapped his raised knee. 'But, you're right, my men,' said he, with a ribald sneer that slowly grew and broke into a great guffaw. 'You're right. I have outflanked the Pilgrims. Pilgrims!' he said with obvious disgust. 'Pilgrims! Conscience and Bible!' He spat out the words. 'They're so soft, they think we're all good honest Englishmen.' He chortled to himself. He slapped his chest. 'I'm a good honest Englishman. I'll help anybody with his burden. I'll lighten the load of any poor, poor Pilgrim.' He opened wide his arms. 'Bring your gold to my friends.' He turned to the sailors. 'Yes my boys,' he said to no one in particular, 'yes my boys, you can congratulate yourselves that you picked up this berth. 'Tis like robbing the blind. 'Tis like taking money from children – from babies.'

He fell silent again. His face clouded. His brow creased, 'But, you drunken fools will ruin all. What – what if one of 'em heard you? Eh? Didn't think of that? No! That never entered your bony heads? No! Well 'tis true you're not paid to think, but to do – to do as you are told. From now on keep your mouths shut tight, do you hear? Do you hear me, Nabal Wilson?' he roared. A nasty smile with no laughter in it came to his lips, 'Do you hear me, Wilson?'

'Yes sir. Yes Master Reynolds, I hear you,' stammered the sailor. 'I hear you, right enough.' He dared not look into his master's blazing eyes.

'Well, do as I say, in future. Get rid of this drink. At once,

I say. Stop this gambling. Up aloft, you lazy idlers. Your work is up above. Keep your lips tight and you shall have your pockets full. D'you follow me? D'you get my meaning?'

'Yes, Master,' came a mumbled reply. 'T'will be just as you say, just as you say.' They picked up their glasses and bottle, slouched across the hold and vanished up the stairs. All was left in total blackness below. Not a light anywhere. Justice and Prudence were all alone – all alone among the sacks and rats. Their ears and hearts throbbed with the words they had just heard. The Pilgrims had been cheated by the captain of the ship! Cheated! And by the captain, himself!

9 *Master Reynolds Brought to Book*

THE children sat quietly for a few moments in the blackness, they were stunned. 'What shall we do?' rushed through their minds. Justice pulled at his sister's apron. They crawled, as silently as they could, over the sacks back to the foot of the stairs. They reached the bottom after stumbling into many mysterious bundles. They listened to the scurrying of the rats about them. Justice felt his heart pounding against his chest, and his hands trembled so that he could hardly hold to the steps. He knew Prudence felt the same. It was with great sighs of relief that they reached the top.

Prudence whispered. 'What shall we do? Oh! it is so frightening, Justice. What can we do? What shall we do?'

'We shall tell Father – straight away,' said Justice sternly. 'We shall have to.'

'But – but we had no right to be down there,' whined his sister. 'We shall be in very serious trouble for going below – dreadful trouble. Father will be very angry with us. We can't say anything. We can't!'

'But we must tell Father. I know – I know we shall be punished – but we must tell Father. We must. We have no choice. He must learn of what we've heard. We can't have our people cheated by the captain.'

They scrambled up the next stairs and reached their parents with all haste. By his time, they had awakened from their shallow, fitful sleep and had begun to wonder about their absent children. 'Where have you been?' demanded their mother. 'I have been so anxious. Why did you not tell us you were going off?'

'You were asleep,' replied Justice sheepishly, his eyes cast to the floor.

'What's the matter, my boy?' questioned his father, standing up. 'Come on! I can see there's trouble afoot. Come on! Tell me all about it. Something's wrong. Where have you been and what have you been doing? You can't hide anything from me.'

Justice shifted from one leg to the other. He tucked in his chin and kept his eyes lowered. He dared not meet his father's piercing glance. He twiddled his fingers nervously.

'Come on, my boy. Speak out!'

Justice opened his mouth. It was dry. Words would not come. He gulped. He licked his lips, nervously. Prudence pulled at his sleeve. 'No Justice, no! We shall be in dreadful trouble.'

He turned to her, 'We must say, we must,' he replied, biting his lower lip.

'What's all this?' said Mr Lovelace. 'What's all this?' 'Trouble? What's the matter, my boy?' He pulled at his son's sleeve. 'Come on – I want to know.' Mr Lovelace put his finger under his son's chin and jerked it upwards. He looked straight into his eyes. 'Tell me.'

Justice began slowly – very slowly – but soon he was blurting out the whole story with a rush. Mr Lovelace heard their story with a grim, serious look set on his face. As the story unfolded his face grew more and more cloudy. 'Right,' he said, when Justice finished. 'Is that it? It's the truth, you've told me?'

'Yes, Father.'

Mr Lovelace caught hold of the low beam above his head. He looked down grimly at the children. They could not decide whether Master Reynolds or they were the object of his unmistakable anger.

'I shall have something to say to you two later – for going

below,' said he, waving his finger at them. 'You have done wrong. Very wrong. You have done wrong to eavesdrop. And soon you shall know the extent of my displeasure. Meanwhile, I have work to do.' He turned sharply. He made straight across the deck to the far corner. Justice and Prudence could hear an indistinct, but animated, conversation. In a short while a group of four Pilgrims had assembled at the bottom of the stairs. Their faces showed their single-mindedness. They had come to a decision – that was plain for all to see. And no one would shake them from it. All had set lips. No smile was to be seen.

Up they climbed, undid the ropes, slid back the hatch and clambered out on to the open deck. The light dazzled their eyes. The wind whistled around them and they saw the white-topped, grey-green seas running high about the little ship. It took their breath away.

Safety lines stretched across the deck. Mr Lovelace pointed towards the captain's cabin. He did not waste his breath in attempting to speak above the howling wind. Instead they bent their heads and made their way aft. Holding on to the ropes, grabbing for very life, they pulled their tortuous, slipping way across to the captain's quarters. Mr Lovelace raised his clenched fist and clouted at the door. Without waiting for a reply, he pushed and went in. The others followed.

Inside the cabin, the captain was seated at his table with a chart spread before him. Another, tall, brightly dressed sailor was standing at his side. Together they were poring over the chart. The opened door allowed in a gust of prying wind which lifted the chart from the table. The captain looked up. 'And who might you be?' he said – slowly. Without pausing for reply, he went on, 'who told you that you could come in here – uninvited, too? Get back to the hold. Keep to your proper place. I can tell you're a Pilgrim,' said he, with undisguised distaste. He made a vague gesture towards the door with his hand. The rings on his fingers sparkled. 'Get

back, I say, all of you – and – and close that door behind you.
Get out! Get out, I say.'

But Mr Lovelace and the three other Pilgrims stood their
ground. 'No, sir, not so fast,' said Mr Lovelace, with steady
voice.

'No, sir?' repeated the captain, lifting his head and slowly
rising from his chair and pushing it back behind him. 'No,
sir? No, sir? What's this? Mutiny I call it. No, sir? You dare

to speak like that to me – No, sir, indeed! And in my own
cabin! And who might you be?' he demanded. 'Who gave
you the right to "No, sir" me, eh? Answer me that.'

'My name is Matthew Lovelace,' came the reply.

'Master Lovelace is it? An' what's your business, Master
Lovelace? What's so pressing – so pressing that you have the
leave to barge into my cabin and deny my orders to my face?
Eh? Tell me that!' As he spoke he prodded his chest. 'My

cabin! My orders! What's your business, you high and mighty Pilgrim?'

Mr Lovelace drew himself up. He breathed in, deeply. 'We shall not be browbeaten by your bluster, my man. We have pressing business to see to. We shall be heard. We've come about the ship. She's leaking.'

'Leaking eh?' The captain threw a pair of dividers down upon the table in disgust. 'Leaking you say. Leaking? What do you expect, man, in a storm like this, may I ask?' he snapped. 'There's water everywhere and you want to know about a leak. Leak indeed! What do you land people know about the sea? Nothing!' He lowered his voice. 'My advice to you, Master Lovelace is that you and your friends stick to your Bible preaching and you leave sailing to those that know.' He sat down at his table and looked up to his gaudy companion. 'What say you, mate?' he challenged.

'Very proper, Master,' came the abject reply. 'Very proper, if I might say so.'

'Enough of this! She's leaking. She's leaking I tell you,' asserted Matthew Lovelace. 'She is leaking.' He paused. He took a deep breath. 'And that's not all – we know your game. We know all about your plans. We know that you don't intend to take us to our new home in America. We know that this vessel is not seaworthy. We know you won't stay with us even though you have promised us a year, if ever you get us there,' he added, wryly. 'You've deceived us long enough, Master Reynolds.'

'You know! You know! What do you know?'

Mr Lovelace advanced towards the captain. He put his hands on to the table and straightened his arms. He looked straight into the captain's eyes. He spoke very slowly and decidedly. ' 'Tis true we know little about sailing, that much I grant you, sir. But we know all about your game. All about it, I say.'

Slowly the colour drained from the captain's face. Then he shook his hand. 'Bluff! Bluff!' he snapped. 'Get out – you land men – you preachers. Get out. There's the way.' He pointed to the door. 'Water everywhere and you say she's leaking,' said he, with unconcealed disgust. 'How far have you sailed before? Tell me that?' he paused. No reply came. 'I thought so.'

'Enough, I say!' interrupted Mr Lovelace. 'You cannot bluff us any more – you know she's leaking and we know your plans. We want this ship made seaworthy. Are you prepared to risk the lives of women and children in this – this floating wreck?'

'Plans. Plans. You know my plans,' Reynolds mimicked. 'How do you know my plans, my clever friend?'

'Nabal Wilson – gaming on the lower deck – not above a half hour ago.' Mr Lovelace spoke deliberately. 'That's how we know your game.' His hand dropped back to his side. The captain fell silent. He exchanged knowing glances with his companion. There was an inward struggle. After a time he began to speak. He spat out the words. 'Nabal Wilson and his drink-driven tongue. I told him – I told him to keep his mouth shut, that drunken swab. He'll pay for this.' He thumped the table. 'He'll pay!'

'So you don't deny it, Master Reynolds? It's true then?' Master Reynolds looked up. He began to tap his fingers on the table. Suddenly, he stood up, angrily pushed his chair aside and paced his cabin. 'Nabal Wilson shall pay for this,' he muttered, punching his cupped left palm with his clenched right fist. 'Yes. He shall pay, that . . . that fool.' He waved his fist wildly. 'He shall pay.'

He regained his seat. He seemed to be in a world of his own. Abruptly, he awoke to the continued presence of the Pilgrims. He tried to stifle his rage. Slowly, an ingratiating smile came to his lips. He looked up. He plucked his ear. He stroked his stubbly chin. 'Well, well. Still here? Ah, well – I'll tell you what I'll do.' He jabbed at the chart. 'Let's see – I'll put her in at Dartmouth for repairs. You can take advice there

– if you will. Yes, yes. Dartmouth will do nicely. I'm an honest man. That's as good an offer as you'll get.'

'Honest man, indeed,' retorted Mr Lovelace. 'Honest? You don't know the meaning of the word, sir.' The four Pilgrims were not to be deceived by the captain's apparently generous air. Had they not discovered his plans? 'Just a moment.' The four black-clothed men retired to a far corner – to discuss the proposition. After a few minutes of whispered animated conversation, they came back to the table. Mr Lovelace spoke. 'Dartmouth will suit us well,' said he. He placed his hands upon the table and leant towards the captain. 'We are simple, plain folk,' he confessed. 'I admit it. I'm glad it is so. But, we have paid decent honest money for your ship and services and we expect a fair bargain. And there is something else I should like to say to you, sir. You should know this – you may try to cheat us – but you will never deceive God. Think of that, sir. You can never deceive God.'

The three other Pilgrims nodded and murmured their agreement. The Pilgrims made such a stark contrast to the captain and his friend. Whilst the Pilgrims were plainly dressed all in black and white, the sailors were richly attired in their finery and were much bejewelled. Mr Lovelace concluded. 'Are we understood? A decent, fair bargain this time, is it?'

'Yes – yes. You have my word,' Reynolds mumbled, with a quick move of his hand.

'I hope your word is to be relied upon.'

The Pilgrims moved to quit the cabin. At the door they stopped and turned back. Mr Lovelace spoke. 'Dartmouth it is then, Master Reynolds. Dartmouth for repairs. And none of your tricks this time – if you please,' he said with emphasis.

The captain said nothing. He merely glowered in reply.

The Pilgrims quietly turned, opened the door and were gone.

10 *Saints and Strangers*

IT was the September of 1620. The Plymouth waterfront was alive with the hustle and bustle of human traffic making preparation for the departure of the *Mayflower*. The Pilgrims no longer had the services of the *Speedwell*. True, there she was – riding the tide out in the bay, anchored near to the *Mayflower*, but the Pilgrims could not be satisfied that she was fit to take them to their desired home. Repairs at Dartmouth had proved a failure. Master Reynolds had demonstrated, yet again, he could not be trusted. As a consequence, some of the Pilgrims had decided to withdraw from the voyage and set up their homes in England. But the rest had made up their minds they would reach Virginia. They were determined to go on. They had already started to transfer their cherished belongings to the *Mayflower* from the near-deserted *Speedwell*.

An armada of tiny boats plied between the two vessels out in the bay, heavy with their precious cargoes. Mr Lovelace stood on the quay with his wife and children.

'Yes,' he said, 'all our stuff must be taken across. We sail on the evening tide.'

'It will be very crowded on the *Mayflower*, won't it, my dear?' said his wife, with obvious concern. 'We were so cramped on the *Speedwell*,' she went on, 'but we shall have even less space now. I know she looks a bigger vessel than the *Speedwell* – I dare say she is bigger – but she certainly needs to be – look how many of us are going to be on board.'

' 'Tis true, what you say, Martha,' agreed her husband

49

with a nod. 'Indeed, we shall be very crowded. There's
something more, though. On this voyage we'll not all be
Pilgrims. We'll have a company of Adventurers going with
us to America.'

'Adventurers, who are they? Do they want the same
freedom of worship as we do?' questioned Justice. 'Is that
why they sail with us?'

'No, my son, they do not, more's the pity. They're not
sailing for religious freedom. Some of them are not at all
religious, for that matter, I'm afraid. Some of them are sailing
just to get away from the proper deserts of their crimes. They
sail to avoid punishment for their wickedness. They prefer a
colony to a prison house.' He gently pulled his children round
to face him. He crouched down to speak confidentially. 'My
children, listen to me. Give me all your attention. We shall
have to be very careful with them on board, I'm afraid,' said
he in a whisper. 'They will not be easy companions, especially
in such close quarters.'

He stood up and gave his children a friendly pat upon their
shoulders. 'I say, do you know what names they are calling
us in the town?' he went on, cheerily. 'Do you know what
they're calling us, the Adventurers and the Pilgrims?' He
gathered his breath. 'Well, we're called the Saints and they're
called the Strangers. What do you think of that? Eh? But
then, God calls his people saints, so 'tis no hardship for us to
bear that name. No! 'Tis our joy.' He stopped and stood,
quietly. He dropped into his thoughts.

Justice and Prudence began to wonder what would befall
them in close cramped company with such people. Their
father's voice broke in upon their fears.

'Let's look upon it as – as an opportunity,' he said.

'An opportunity? An opportunity for what, Father?'

'Why,' he said, 'an opportunity to show the gospel by our
lives, of course. Look at it this way. Let's hope that some of
them will come to our times of worship on board. Some of
them will hear the preaching of God's Word in that way. And

that's not all. They'll see us day by day. They'll see us under all sorts of conditions. Maybe they start this voyage as those who have no interest in spiritual things – Strangers, indeed – but who can tell whether God shall call them by his grace? Who knows but he has planned to do that very thing? We must pray that God will call many of them to become his saints as they travel across the sea. Strangers can be made Saints, by God's grace.'

The menfolk among the Pilgrims took their responsibilities very seriously indeed. Mr Lovelace was no exception. He accepted his obligations as the head of the family and earnestly tried to fulfil them. He gathered his family before him and counselled them that they should show much courage and patience on the voyage. He told them, 'We must expect and bear the hardship that we are bound to meet. Much meekness must be shown. Let us show true humility – in this way,' he said, 'we may hope that we shall be a commendation of the gospel of our Lord Jesus Christ.'

11 'Goodbye, England!'

IT was early evening that same day. The last day in England for the Pilgrims. They had settled in their new quarters on board the *Mayflower*. The Lovelaces had spent a frustrating time below, setting up home once again, in even more cramped conditions than before. At the earliest possible moment they had gone on deck for welcome fresh air. Now, they were pressed hard against the ship's side, looking back towards the shore. Pilgrim families were all around them. The deck was bustling with the activity of the sailors. All was shouts, whistles and movement aboard. Unintelligible orders rang out. In quick response, bare-footed men sprang, cat-like, into the rigging. Their arms pulled away with a will on the sheets. Their wriggling bodies started to ascend. Up and up they climbed. Justice thought they surely must lose their grip and fall from the rigging to be dashed upon the deck or plunged down into the sea. But no! Sure-footed, up and up they climbed, until those at the top seemed like tiny specks in the pale blue sky. Prudence had to shield her eyes against the sun as she lifted her face to stare in amazement at their lurchings in the topmost rigging. Her heart throbbed within her as she saw the men shuffling their precarious way out across the yards.

As the children gazed upward, another mysterious, strident order rang from the boatswain. Immediately, the windlass started to run, squealing its resistance. The ropes strained and began to pull at the anchor. All of a sudden – away she came! Away she came from her last muddy grip on England. The

52

Mayflower was free! She started to drift in the swelling tide. At once, another command was given and the men in the rigging let go the sails. They fell, uncoiling at a furious pace. The lines were made fast around the cleats. Almost at once the wind filled the billowing canvas. The *Mayflower* lurched into the tide. Justice heard the familiar creaking of the boards start up, once again. He felt the deck move beneath his feet.

'We're off,' he said to Prudence. 'We're off.'

The children were tense with excitement – their breath held within them and their arms and legs tight. Mr Lovelace called them to order.

'My children,' he said, 'come – take your long last look at England. You will never see her again.'

The children stood still. No words passed their lips. They listened to the deep, steady voice of their father.

'That is the land of your birth, my children,' he said, raising his arm and pointing back towards the shore. 'You'll never see it again.' He paused, 'God pity that land.' He stopped, looked back to the shore, but said nothing. After what seemed an endless time of gazing back at the shore, the spell was broken. Mr Lovelace slowly tapped the wooden rail with his fingers. He began to speak again. The children were just able to catch his low-toned words. He was thinking aloud. 'May King James see sense,' he said, keeping time with his drumming beat. 'May King James see sense, before it is too late.'

The children looked up – quizzically – into the face of their father. They saw tears in his eyes. They glistened in the evening sun as he turned his head away. Thin, watery lanes began to appear down his cheeks. Mr Lovelace put his arm about his wife and held her close, with Justice and Prudence standing between them. The four of them hugged themselves against the side of the ship, as the *Mayflower* dipped her bowsprit, picked up speed and headed out into the open sea. They lingered over their last, long look back at England. 'We will never see her again. Never!' They stayed there until their

eyes strained to keep hold of their beloved homeland. It grew
more and more difficult to distinguish the land from the
greyness of the sea and the lowering sky.

It was gone! They woke up with a kind of start. 'That's it,
then,' said Mr Lovelace. 'Come, my dears, we've left England.
Left England for good. Let's go forward to the bows and look
towards the West. That's where our home lies now. There
lies the only home we shall have in this world.'

They made their way forward, picking their steps amidst
the tangle of ladders, spars, barrels and pumps that cluttered
the deck. The prow was dipping into the ocean and slowly
rising again. The keen wind blew about them. They felt the
salt spray caress them – but this was no storm. The wind and
sea were too gentle for that, far too gentle. Justice sensed the
excitement tingling in his limbs. 'We're off. This is it, then.

At last, we have turned our backs upon England and all its persecution.'

Mr Lovelace seemed to echo the thoughts of his son. 'King James said he would harry us out of the land. He has, too. It should never be necessary for us to hazard our lives like this – to get freedom of worship.' They raised their eyes to the West. They looked on the setting sun in the far distance. The sky was all a gentle, glorious red.

'Fine weather tomorrow,' said Mrs Lovelace.

'How do you know, Mother?'

'Red sky at night, shepherds' and sailors' delight, Prudence, my dear.'

'That proverb is very old,' took up Mr Lovelace. 'Jesus said that the people knew it, even in his day.'

The dying orb grew redder and larger. It was slowly but surely falling from the sky to sink beneath the waves. The sea and sky were all aflame. The great red ball began to disappear beneath the placid mill-pond. A column of fire ran along the unruffled, flat-topped ocean, up the bowsprit to meet them in the ship. The spars, rigging and sails were all set alight. The Lovelaces stood in the bows, gazing at the vanishing sun. They gazed and gazed without saying a word, until it finally and silently disappeared beneath the waves. But the sun had not yet given up its hold of the day. It struggled to maintain its fiery grip over the sky. A hazy, dusky red glow filled the heavens. But gradually the creeping, approaching night put out the flames. The sun was extinguished. Night had commenced its reign.

'Come, Martha,' said Mr Lovelace, gently pulling his wife around with one arm and clutching hold of Justice and Prudence with the other. 'Come, my loves, let's go below. Let's get to our sleep. We're on our way to our new home, this time.'

They turned towards the hatchway and strolled across the deck, slowly and steadily rising and falling in the gentle sea. They paused, they stood to listen to the unfamiliar songs of the sailors, making fast the sheets for the night. They saw other Pilgrim families, much as their own, standing around in little knots by the side of the ship.

They gently moved on. They reached the hatch that led below to their quarters. They stood at the top of the hatchway. They stopped and took a last look round. Then they set foot on the steps. The children went first. Mr Lovelace took off his great black hat, lowered his head, and he, with his wife, disappeared from view.

12 *Long Dreamy Days*

THE long warm days of late Summer passed quickly into early Autumn. Of course, not all days were balmy. Some days a hostile rain spattered the ship. At other times, a sharp, nipping wind poked its unwelcome, keen nose into every crevice. It spoke ominously of icy, wintry days to come. On other days, a dank drizzle covered the ship. The children found those days greatly to their liking. They loved to peer out of the hatches to see the wondrous effect the water droplets had upon the ship. They were infatuated by the moistened wooden spars as they glistened in the watery light and revealed their many shades of red and brown. It seemed that the colours were two shy to display their charms, except on those damp mornings. The water drops hung like sparkling diamonds on the ropes and they held much fascination for the children. The decks shone and all that was dull and bland when dry sprang into a veritable kaleidoscope of colour. The *Mayflower* bejewelled herself upon those damp days.

But in the main, the days were long and warm. Amiable days, they were. Justice and Prudence took advantage of the long dreamy afternoons. They found a spot near the bows that came to be their favourite haunt for many happy hours at a stretch. It really belonged to a friendly ship's carpenter, who stored his tools in the long, low locker there. But the children treated it as their own – their very own. They delighted to sit there in the sunny afternoons. They would press their backs against friendly coils of rope whilst the high sides of the ship sheltered them from the force of the wind.

They spent many carefree afternoon hours there idly talking over the events of the voyage. They soon looked like regular seafarers, for their faces quickly browned by reason of the sun and wind upon them. How happy they were in those days! What long pleasant afternoons they whiled away!

True, they had found their nights a difficult experience.

'Do you find those blankets we have, rough, Justice?' said Prudence.

'Yes, I do,' he answered, emphatically. 'They make my face itch. They're so rough. But that's not the worst thing to me – about sleeping, I mean,' he added with feeling. 'I find the hard pillow I have for my head the worst thing. The blankets are bad – but the pillow is awful!'

'Oh, Justice, that is naughty of you to say such a thing,' replied Prudence, sharply. 'Remember, you know Mother told you not to complain about the pillow. She said that you were far better off than Jacob. She reminded you that he only had a stone for his pillow. You know she warned you not to grumble again.'

'Yes, I know,' he replied. He paused. 'But you're no better yourself,' he snapped. 'You're no different. You complained about the hard deck. Mother had to get you an old sack to sleep on. So I don't see how you can criticize me.'

'You know I'm thinner than you,' responded Prudence. 'My bones stick out and I feel the boards more than you do. Anyway, don't let's quarrel.'

'No,' agreed her brother. 'Father would be very cross if he heard us. He never complains, does he?'

They fell silent for a few moments. 'No – never. He never complains. Nor does Mother.' Words failed the children. They fell silent, each absorbed with their own thoughts.

Prudence broke the silence. 'I wonder what it will be like – in America – I mean,' she said. The look in her eyes and the tone of her voice showed that, in her mind, she had travelled far beyond their place in the bows of the *Mayflower* to that distant, unknown but beckoning land.

'Father told me we shall have a log cabin for a home,' said Justice, with authority. 'At least, after we have cut the wood from the forest and built it, I mean.' A far-away look came into his eyes, too.

Just then an intruder's voice broke in upon their thoughts. 'America, is it? Do you wish to hear about America?'

They looked up and saw a kindly-looking sailor gazing down upon them. It was their affable carpenter. His gentle voice spoke of his friendly ways.

'Have you been there?'

'Been there? I should say I have. Time and again. D'you want to hear about it?'

'Yes, please, sir.'

'Make way then. Make way. Let me have some room.' The children moved over and he squatted down beside them. 'Right snug you've got it here, ain't you?' he said with a smile. 'Right cosy, ain't it? Well then, America. Where shall I begin? I know! Well now. Let's see. Have you heard of the Great Auk? Eh? Tell me that.'

'Great what?' chorused the children in disbelief.

'Great Auk. Oh! you ain't, eh? Well, then, the Great Auk is a bird – see. What's special about it is – it can't fly!'

The children laughed. 'Can't fly? A bird that can't fly?'

'That's right, a bird that can't fly. Mind you, it's good to eat.'

'A bird that can't fly? You're teasing us.'

'No. I'm not, 'onest. But like I said, it's good to eat, even if it ain't good at flying. You'll see. Then there's wild strawberries, enormous sweet potatoes and, o' course, wild turkey. Roast turkey's lovely, I can tell you.'

'I wish we had some now. What else is there?'

'Anything else? O' course there is. Let me see now. Yes. There's great river trout to fish for and eat and – ah, yes – oysters. Fair makes your mouth water to think of it. Oysters.'

'Oysters? What's oysters?'

'Oysters? Why, bless you, oysters is . . . Why, oysters is . . . oysters o' course. Well, let's see, they're shell fish. You slips your knife into 'em, see, split 'em open and then you have a dish fit for a king. That's oysters. Fit for a king it is.'

The children by now were completely engrossed. 'What else is there, sir?'

'What else? What else? you ask. Why, let me see. Well now, the whole place is filled – at the right time of the year, mind you – with the wonderful smell of magnolia. A sweet scent it is. Fills all the air it does. Perfume fit for a queen, that is.'

'What about the Indians, sir? Are there Red Indians in America? I've heard people say there are wild men there.'

'Red Indians? Red Indians, you say. I've seen 'undreds of 'em, my lad, 'undreds. Red Skins, 'eathen savages. Fierce they be – with feathers on their 'eads and down their backs. Funny paintings on their faces, too. Ah! And when they 'oops and 'ollers, it fair makes your blood go cold and curdle inside you. Makes your legs go all of a wobble, like. Turns your 'eart to water, it does. Keep you awake at night that will, my lad. Ah! Then, o'course, there's the packs of fiercesome wild creatures in the great forests. Untamed they be. Oh, America – you'll love that great land. But look 'ere, I've got me job to do. The captain won't thank me for sitting about talking like a woman. I must be off and about my duties.'

He stood up to leave. He looked down at the children.

'Thank you, sir. Thank you for telling us about our new home.'

'That's nothing, my boy. Think nothing of it. I'll be right glad to get there meself. Turkey and sweet potatoes with a dish of wild strawberries. Fit for a king, that is.' He rubbed his stomach, and off he went with a hearty chuckle. The children heard him as he moved away. 'Fit for a king, that is. Fit for a king.'

The children said nothing for a long while. They sat dreaming – dreaming of their new home. 'Oysters. What *were* they? . . . And a bird that couldn't fly? . . . Sweet potatoes? . . .'

Prudence was the first to speak. Her thoughts returned to sterner matters of no beds and no mattresses. Present discomforts were more real to her than future pleasures, however inviting and rosy they had been made to appear.

'I hope – I hope I shall have a feather pillow and clean sheets and a straw mattress to sleep upon,' she said, all in a rush.

'Yes, so do I,' agreed Justice with sympathetic fellow-feeling. 'I've just about had enough of hard planks.'

They fell silent and continued to muse of the happy days ahead of them. It eased their present pains to think of future joys. In their dreams, they left the harsh world of hard boards, rough pillows and coarse blankets far, far behind. Whilst they dreamed, the ship ploughed on and on towards the land of the Great Auk, oysters and wild strawberries. The land of the great forests and the wild Red Skins.

'I wish we did not have to have lessons, don't you?' Justice broke into his sister's dreams. Every morning, apart from Sundays, Mrs Lovelace took the children and made them work at their lessons. They had to learn their letters and master the spelling book. Their father sometimes would come to stand by them as they sat at their work. He listened to their answers. He said little, but watched, with just a suggestion of a smile playing about his lips as the children screwed their faces and chewed their tongues in concentration. Now and then he would bend over to give a brief word of encouragement at some particularly good effort, or frown

61

slightly – very slightly – at some simple mistake (of which there were not a few).

'It's very difficult to write straight, isn't it?' said Prudence. 'I mean, every time the ship heaves over I make a dreadful mess on my book.'

'Yes, that's right,' agreed her brother. 'And I can't spell so well when the ship keeps moving up and down,' he added.

'That's silly – how can a moving ship make you spell wrong? That's just silly to say that.'

'Oh, is it? Well it's true. So there!'

In addition to their letters, Mrs Lovelace made their children work at sums. That was a heavy burden for the children to carry. Sums! Also she made them read to her, especially from the Bible. She made them learn the facts of history and geography. Above all, she taught them Scripture knowledge. In common with all the children of the Pilgrims, Justice and Prudence were regularly catechized. Their parents took time, each day, to question the children on their knowledge of the Bible. By questions and answers the children came to learn its teaching. They came to know it well. They had been taught this way, for as long as they could remember.

'I like the geography of America, don't you?' said Prudence.

'Yes. That is interesting.'

Prudence had not forgotten the talk about the Red Indians. 'Do you think we *shall* find Indians there?'

'Yes. We shall. Father told me.'

'I wonder if they will be savage and fight us?'

'I expect they will, but we'll be all right – we have plenty of muskets.' He paused. 'But I heard Father talking with some of the others the other day and know they hope they won't have to fight the Indians. I know Father hopes to take the gospel to them. He was telling Mother he hopes we can all live together happily.'

Once again the children fell back into dreaming. They gazed vaguely into the distance. Very often they fell to wondering, as they lazed the hours away in the warm early autumnal sun.

Inevitably, however, their pleasant dreams were interrupted by the recurring remembrance of present discomforts. One such affliction that often figured in their discussions was their food. Day after day the Pilgrims had little change in their diet. Dry biscuits, so hard – salt beef, so tough and salty. And, above all, the thick vegetable gruel. 'Oh, to have fresh-picked fruit again,' said Prudence. 'Won't it be lovely – just to bite into a nice crunchy, juicy apple?' After weeks at sea the fruit had long given out.

'Well – I would like some real meat,' said her brother.

'What do you mean, real meat? The salt beef *is* real meat.'

'I know it is, but I mean fresh roast meat. This salt meat is so dry and so hard,' he added. 'My teeth and gums ache so, with the biscuits and the tough beef. Real jaw breakers they are.'

'I'm glad it is so dark down below, especially when we eat.'

'Yes. So am I.' Justice heartily agreed.

Both of them well understood their mutual satisfaction at eating in such dim light. After a time at sea, the food was alive with crawling weevils. 'The one good thing about the dark,' said Justice, 'is that you don't have to see what you eat.'

'Nor drink,' added Prudence. She did not need to spell out her meaning. The drinking water had long become foul, green and scummy.

Another far-away look came into Prudence's eyes. The children preferred to dwell on more pleasant matters. 'We shall have turkey, newly roasted, in America . . . Justice, think of Mother's bread and cakes again. Do you remember those days – oh, they seem so long ago now – when Mother used to make that fresh, warm bread and those hot cakes and gave them to us straight from the oven? Do you remember them? Do you remember how we used to sit, sometimes, in the stairs over the kitchen and dangle our feet in the warm air? Can you remember the warm, inviting smell of fresh bread,

Justice? And do you remember the taste of that lovely, crusty bread? How good it was. Oh! Oh! to have some warm fresh bread now, this very minute.'

'It seems so long ago – I've almost forgotten it.'

'I haven't. I shall remember it for – for ever. I shall. I know I shall. Oh! I could eat some of it now.'

'It would be good. Yes – and you wouldn't need to eat it with your eyes closed!'

As the days passed, the voyage grew more and more irksome. Washing in the mornings was a very real problem. There was the burden of trying to get to the water butts when everyone else had the same idea. There was precious little privacy. None at all, in fact. But that was not the worst of it. Another and greater aggravation was the long queue. Justice, in his impatience, once tried to wash in salt sea water. He had grown tired of the wait for fresh. 'Fresh, is it?' he murmured. 'Fresh! With all this scum in it? I can't wait. I won't wait.' So he went to use sea water – but he quickly learned his lesson.

'You know Father told you not to wash in the sea water,' remonstrated his sister, when she saw him.

Justice needed no second telling. The redness and the soreness of his eyes gave him all the reminders he needed. He'd wait in future for the foul, but non-salty washing water.

The children came on deck whenever they could, as did all the other passengers. The cramped and airless conditions below soon made the air stale and the stench proved almost unbearable. The noxious smell of half-poisoned air, breathed already by others a dozen times, made them feel sick. The foul stench was increased by the smell of rancid tallows, unwashed bodies, stale fetid food and the damp musty odour of blankets wet through with the continual drip of sea water. The children came to hate the foul damp of the vile, swarming hold. The offensive air pressed against their chests, so that they could hardly breathe. There was no room to play, to run or jump. There was no light by which to see. It was horrible. The stinking, shadowy cellar was almost a prison to them.

They hated the long weary days when they were compelled to stay below because of the weather. 'It's a proper dungeon and no mistake.' Whenever it was possible they came above. The children loved to feel the breeze in their hair and the spray upon their faces. They loved to hear the gentle singing of the sea and to breathe the clear fresh air. So it was that many, many happy hours were spent in their special secret place near the bows. That was the only bearable place on board.

However, little could they imagine what was in store for them . . .

13 *Tempest*

ABRUPTLY, all was changed. One day – that had started fine enough – in the mid-afternoon, the wind began to pick up from the West and the seas began to rise. The sailors gloomily predicted a squall. The poor tiny cork of a ship began to bob upon the increasingly choppy waters. The leaden clouds brooded overhead.

Mr Lovelace spoke to his children. 'A heavy storm will be upon us before nightfall,' he warned. 'We must spend the afternoon in lashing all things below as securely as we can. You must on no account venture above decks. You understand me, Justice? None of your tricks now! These waves can catch you unawares and once you have been sucked over – well – there's precious little chance of being brought back. That'll be the finish of you. You understand? Both of you?'

'Yes, Father.'

'You'll stay below?'

'Yes, Father. We promise.'

The Pilgrims spent the next hours in making their possessions safe. All the while, the wind was rising. As they worked, they could hear it screaming through the rigging. Justice and Prudence took a last look at the sea and sky before they finally went below. They observed the wind chasing the blackening, looming clouds across the wild sky and whipping up the sea into a white froth above its heaving, grey swell. The captain gave the order for all sails to be shortened and the hatches to be closed. The sailors hastened to obey. Justice stood upon the steps as the hatches were battened down. He

watched the sea begin to break over the side of the ship. He
heard the thunder-like roar of the waves as they dashed
themselves upon the decks. Those friendly decks, so familiar
in the long sunny afternoons, now took on a treacherous and
grim air of hostility. He caught a glimpse of the special spot
of quiet rest, where he and Prudence had spent so many happy
hours. He saw the bows of the ship plunge beneath the waves
and he knew their private haunt had just been covered by tons
of salt water. 'If we had been sitting there!' He shuddered at
the very thought.

Bang! Crash! Down slammed the hatches. Suddenly – at
once – all was blackness below to his eyes until, gradually he
could begin to distinguish (but with much difficulty) the

huddled groups of bewildered and apprehensive men and women. 'What is going to happen?'

The captain came into the dungeon-like hold. He beckoned with his hand for silence and stillness. Those standing looked around for a space to sit. The commotion gradually died down – that is, the human commotion. A hush came upon them – a hush brought by fear. Justice could still hear the roar of the sea and wind outside. 'My friends,' the captain said. 'I will be honest with you, I think that it is right that you should know what is coming. We're in for a very heavy and violent storm. We've taken in all sail,' he went on, 'and I've put my most able helmsman at the wheel – lashed him there to hold her into the wind. Now, I must have your co-operation. I have enough work to do above, without the added trouble of looking after curious passengers. Under no circumstances must any of you venture out on to the main deck. The seas will make it all awash very soon. I can't guarantee your safety aloft. I appeal to you. No! more that that – I command you. Do not disobey me. Don't! I know life is very hard for you down here. I cannot say how long you will be shut in below. I know it's not very pleasant, but however difficult and painful it is – I beseech you – if you value your lives – stay below whilst the storm lasts. Stay below! Am I understood, my friends?' he challenged finally, looking around the company. 'Am I understood?'

One of the Pilgrim fathers spoke for them all. 'You need have no fears, sir,' he answered. 'We understand your meaning. We are prepared for hardship. By God's help there will be no panic. We're a law-abiding people. We shall submit. We shall comply with your rules.'

'Very well. I'm heartily pleased to hear it. You'll make my work far easier by staying below – to say nothing of preserving your own lives. Now, my friends, I have much work to do above. So, if there are no questions, I'll be going above.' No one said anything. 'Very well.' The captain left the hold to make his way back to his quarters. Before the people dispersed,

Mr Lovelace called out. 'Let's join in prayer. Let's commit ourselves to God.'

'You lead us, Matthew,' came a voice from a murky corner. 'You lead us.'

'So be it – if that's your wish.'

There was a general murmur of assent. Mr Lovelace stood up and struggled across to the main beam. He clutched hold of it to keep himself steady. He solemnly addressed the whole company.

'Before we pray,' he said, 'I should like to remind you all of some comforts from the Lord. Comforts for our minds to help us in this coming tempest. You've just heard, my friends, that we are in great danger; well, our God is greater than our danger. Remember that, will you? Remember how Christ stilled the tempest in his days. Remember that our God is the sovereign God of earth and sky and sea. Think of it, my friends, during the terrifying hours of this great storm that may be coming upon us. Let us all remember the word of our God.' He paused, then went on quoting from the twenty-ninth Psalm, as he did. 'Ascribe to the LORD, O mighty ones, ascribe to the LORD glory and strength. Ascribe to the LORD the glory due to his name; worship the LORD in the splendour of his holiness. The voice of the LORD is over the waters; the God of glory thunders, the LORD thunders over the mighty waters. The voice of the LORD is powerful; the voice of the LORD is majestic . . . The LORD sits enthroned over the flood; the LORD is enthroned as King for ever. The LORD gives strength to his people; the LORD blesses his people with peace.' The roar of the elements outside gave added meaning to his speech. With many other solemn words he encouraged the company. He exhorted them to have confidence in their God. Having finished his address to the people, he said, 'Now let us all pray.' Gravely, and with no hint of fear or trembling, he began. He called upon God for his protection. He asked for deliverance of the vessel and all within it. He worshipped and adored God for his great power and he blessed him for his many and faithful promises. All the Pilgrims joined in a heartfelt, 'Amen' as he closed his prayer. Justice, seated in the corner, added his own weak and trembling voice to that of his fellows. But, in his heart, he was afraid. He felt his heart beating against his chest. He knew he was going to cry. He desperately wanted to be brave – brave like his father. But he could not help himself. Tears began to flow down his face. He began to sob.

Prudence, also, tried to bite her lip, to hold back her tears. But, she could not restrain herself, either. Down the tears flowed. She, too, began to heave and sob. Almost at once, the children felt the strong arms of their father about them. He tenderly drew them to himself and soon the whole family was huddled together in their corner of the hold. The children marvelled that their father could be so strong – so solemn whilst in prayer and yet so tender in his affection towards them. Justice tried to stop his crying. He was sobbing now, without tears. He began to feel sick, violently sick. He heard the cries of others, all around him. He glanced out into the gloom. But soon, even this din was drowned by the pounding of the huge seas on to the deck above. The ship was awash, he knew it. She was being battered; bashed to pieces, perhaps. The Pilgrims were in almost total darkness. The air was foul. The place was vile. It was suffocating. All of them, men, women, and children, were sickened by the continual heaving of the ship. They did not know, nor did they care, whether it was night or day.

But they were reasonably dry. Mothers comforted their children. The men strengthened and encouraged their wives. Above all, they were confident in God. The Lord was with them. He blessed his people with peace. Soon, all were overcome by sheer exhaustion and they fell into a troubled sleep only to be awakened from time to time by the violent motion of the ship and the continual howling of the storm.

14 John Howland

THE next day dawned, but the Pilgrims did not realize it
had. The new dawn came but brought no respite from
the violence of the storm. In their dismal coop, the Pilgrims
gradually awoke, not appreciating that it was day. One by
they grasped that they were still to be confined to the
blackness of the hold below – maybe for a long time to come.
Their trouble was not yet over.

Justice spoke with trembling voice to his sister. 'How do
you feel?' he managed to say.

'Awful,' she replied. 'It's hard to breathe . . . my head
aches. My stomach hurts. The smell is horrible. Oh for
air! . . . oh for air to breathe.'

Many of the Pilgrims felt the same, but they knew they
dared not open up the hatches. The water was a torrent above
them. It was impossible to go up. The captain had warned
them of the danger. They knew that they would be washed
overboard and be drowned at once – and – what of the hold?
It would – most likely – be filled with water and drown them
all below. Whatever the agony, they just had to stay below.
They had to.

'Lie still, my children.' The soft, consoling voice of their
half-asleep mother encouraged them. 'Lie still. If you rebel
against the storm you will find yourself hurt the more. Lie
still, until it has passed.'

Justice glanced around him. He seemed to be the only one
with his head raised. No! There was another. He dimly saw
one of the men, whom he recognized as Mr John Howland,

struggle and stand up. Mr Howland laboriously pulled his slow, dragging way across the hold. He made for the steps. Justice wondered what he was going to do. 'Where is he going?' Mr Howland reached the bottom of the steps. He began to climb.

Justice cried out. 'No! Mr Howland! No! don't go up, Mr Howland. Don't, Mr Howland!'

'Silence, boy!' came the stern reply. 'I must have air. D'you hear me, I must have air. I cannot breathe. This foul stench is killing me. I must breathe.'

'No! Sir! No, sir,' cried Justice. 'Don't open the hatches. Please. Please.'

'I will, boy. Keep still and be silent,' he shouted back.

By now, many had been roused and were sitting up to see what the commotion was about.

'Mr Howland's going up to the main deck,' cried Justice. 'He's going to open the hatches.'

Hands reached out to grab Mr Howland. But he slipped their grasp. He pulled back the hatches and went out.

By now, Mr Lovelace was fully awakened. He called to some other men near him. He grabbed wildly at a rope and his frenzied hands soon had it fastened about his waist. 'Tie the other end to the mast,' he bawled. He spat upon his hands and furiously rubbed them together. 'Quick, man! Quick, man!' He snatched up a great boat-hook that lay in the centre of the hold and madly scrambled up the steps after Mr Howland.

As he got out on to the deck, all he could see was a great wall of water. Where was Mr Howland? He was gone! No! there he was! He could just pick out Mr Howland – struggling wildly in the sea. He had been washed over, as soon as he had appeared on deck. But he had managed to grab hold of a rope. As Mr Lovelace stood there, the ship heaved into the waves and Mr Howland disappeared into the wall of water. Then, as the ship came out of the depths, he was flung clear again. He was still there! Mr Lovelace saw him. He frantically thrust the hook out towards him in desperation. But he missed him, slipped, lost his footing and slithered across the deck. He crashed into the side of the ship which beat all the air out of his body. Miraculously, he had retained his hold of the hook.

Mr Lovelace pulled himself off the deck and clutched the side. Once again, he saw Mr Howland as the ship rose out of the water. He thrust the hook at him again. 'I must get him. Let me get him, O Lord. Let me get him, please.' And he did. This time he caught the half-drowned man. A watcher standing at the hatch saw what had happened. 'Pull! Pull for your life,' he yelled below. 'Pull!'

Unseen men within the hold pulled with all their might on the rope. The pair on deck were dragged, half-drowned to the hatchway and yanked down the steps. There they lay – in a collapsed, bedraggled bundle at their foot. The hatches were heaved together again and securely lashed.

Mr Lovelace quickly recovered. True he was drenched through with icy water. But he soon was his normal self. He looked down at his icy hands with a kind of shock. They had lost all feeling, but he saw that they were red raw, and blood covered. He had not realized how he had cut himself and burned his hands on the rope. As his hands thawed, the pain grew more and more intense. Mr Howland, however, did not revive so easily. He lay in a violent paroxysm – coughing and spitting for a long time. It was many minutes before he had recovered well enough even to sit up with his back against the steps. Still he coughed – deep, painful coughs.

'You stupid man!' The cries of the people greeted him. 'You stupid man! You could have cost us our lives – all of us. And Matthew nearly lost his, and if the water had got below, the whole ship would have gone down at once. You stupid man! Why did you do it? We promised the captain – you stupid man.'

One of the Pilgrim Fathers stood up and addressed the crowd. 'Let this serve as a warning to us all. We gave our word to the captain. This man,' said he, pointing at Mr Howland, 'this man has brought us into disrepute by breaking our word. Look you here,' he went on, raising his voice, 'it might seem unbearable here below – I know it is – we can all feel how cramped we are. The suffocation is horrible. Nobody enjoys the foul air. Nobody enjoys being caged like this. But we do not venture out on any account. Is that understood? We stay below!'

There was no sound from the people.

'I say – is it understood? Answer me!'

A low murmur of agreement followed.

Justice listened to them in silence. He whispered to his sister. 'We must stick it, Prudence. We must stick it. We must!'

The sickening voyage continued. The sea pummelled them from below and battered them from above. She seemed intent on breaking in upon them, in one way or another. The *Mayflower* continued her violent lurching. She would be lifted out of the water one minute and then be dropped down into the depths. With relief, she would struggle back to the uneasy surface. The sea, with malicious intent, lifted her bodily, rolled her wildly as though to break her back, and then in disgust, flung her aside with great violence. The wind added its power, whipping the sea and rain and hurling the massive water broadside against her.

Meanwhile in the darkness below, the families tried to settle down once again. Eyelids grew heavy. Voices grew muffled and thick. Gradually, comforting sleep gave a welcome respite to the people. They fell into gentle, inviting unconsciousness. Oblivion took over. As the Pilgrims slept, the *Mayflower* pursued her wild, drunken course. She and all her helpless prisoners were, by now, many, many leagues off their intended course. They were battered, bewildered and lost upon the trackless, untamed and unforgiving ocean.

15 *The Jack-Screw*

A FEW punishing hours passed. The passengers slept on. Then, Justice was awakened – with a start. Water – icy water – was pouring in upon him.

'Wake up! Wake up!' he shouted. He shook his father, frantically. His mother and Prudence stirred. Another blast of icy cold water poured in upon them.

The commotion aroused the whole company. 'What is it?' came the muffled cry from the murky gloom.

'The force of the gale has opened the main seam of the deck,' replied Mr Lovelace. 'Look here,' he shouted. 'Look here.' He pointed up by the main beam. He held a lantern in his hand. He directed the light up to the roof and they could see the water seeping in. 'Look, Father,' said Justice, pointing up to the main beam, 'look at the beam. Look at the beam . . .' His voice trailed off.

'What, my son? What is it? Where is it?'

'Here, Father. Here.'

The light was moved in closer. The hold was wide awake now. 'What is it?' came a dozen voices, in anxious chorus.

'I see, I see,' said Mr Lovelace. 'I see it. It's pulling out. The weight of the water is forcing the main beam out of place. Look here,' said he, pointing to the trouble. 'Do you see it?'

'That we do.'

They heard the splitting creak as well as saw the widening crack.

'If this goes on,' came a voice, 'we shall be torn in two. We're pulling apart.'

75

'We shall drown – we shall drown.'

'Or else perish in the icy blast,' cried another.

'Keep calm. Don't panic.'

'How can we hold her together?'

'Send for the captain,' came a yell. 'We must send for the captain. Why d'you stand there gawping at a crack that might send us to the bottom? Send for the captain.'

After what seemed an age of waiting by the uneasy Pilgrims, the captain at last stood before them. He was silent. Dour, he examined the beam. One of the men held a lantern close by the trouble. Not a word passed his grim-set lips. At last, his hands fell down by his side. He sighed – deeply. He turned to face the Pilgrims.

'Well, what's it to be?'

'We're done for, my friends. We're done for,' said he, very quietly and slowly. 'I feared this might happen. I'm afraid the sea has broken her back. She's had enough. She's an old ship – she can take no more of this. I said it would be á violent storm. The sea has forced this beam – here – out of place.' As he spoke he pointed to the growing crevice. He gently patted the offending place. Slowly but surely the gap was widening.

'What's to do?' One man voiced a score of thoughts.

The captain raised his hand. 'I'm afraid, my friends – I'm afraid to say we have only a few more minutes left.'

'Never!' came a chorus of disbelief. 'A few minutes?'

The captain had to raise his hand once more, to subdue the noise. 'It's true, I tell you. See now – the beam is still moving. Here 'tis.' He held the lantern up to the joist, 'See – it's cracking and splitting. A few more minutes and we shall be done for, I tell you.'

'Can't we force her back?' a shaky lone voice asked.

'Force it back? Well – 'tis possible – I suppose.' The captain fell silent and thoughtfully scratched his chin. 'But – we don't have the tools with us.' His hand went to his hair and he scratched wildly at it. 'Tools! Tools! If only we had the tools.

If only . . . Bricks need straw and this job needs tools.' He punched the air, wildly.

'Can't we push it back?'

'Push it back? I wish we could. But – it'll take more strength than we've got, I'm afraid, my friend.'

'Well, let's try. Let's try. Anything's better than sitting about here, waiting to go down – surely?' A sea of anxious faces surrounded the captain.

'Impossible! Face facts, men – we're done for. We're beaten. 'Tis only a question of time.'

'No. No, that cannot be! There must be something we can do.'

'I tell you, we're done for.'

A Pilgrim pushed up to the captain and gripped his coat, two-fisted. He tugged in time with his words. 'There must be something we can do.'

'Get off, man. Get off – this is no use.' The captain shoved away the man. He smoothed himself. 'Listen, will you? All of you. She's breaking up. We're finished.'

Children cried. 'Lost. Broken . . .' Women looked anxiously at the husbands. 'What will happen? Are we finished?'

Panic was on the verge of breaking out. Then, a voice came from a far corner of the hold. 'Will my old iron jack-screw do the job?'

'What's that?' cried the captain turning to the corner from whence he had heard the question. He pushed his way through the crowd and reached the speaker. 'What did you say? Your iron jack-screw – you've brought along a jack-screw? I don't recall seeing one come on board – nor on the list.'

'Well, mine's down below – in the stores. I can assure you of that,' came the reply.

'Well, that's the only answer,' said the captain. 'A jack-screw. Quick!' he called. 'Quick! Down men. Down and get it. At once! At once! Do you hear?'

There was a mad scramble of feet as men made for the steps

that led down to the storehold. 'The jack-screw – get the jack-screw. Quick! No delay there! Out of my way . . .' The sound of their feet clattered down the steps as they rushed to get the screw – the screw they hoped would mean their salvation. An uneasy silence fell upon the hold – broken only by feet pacing the floor and the anxious tapping of fingers. There was much biting of lip and quick repeated glances at the beam. Rapid snatches of irritable conversation broke out to give way to silence once more. After a seemingly interminable wait the men were back with their precious, strange treasure.

With much heaving, pulling and twisting the great screw was pulled up the stairs, dragged across the hold and raised to the beam. Willing hands clamped it in place. Almost immediately a man began to twist its great arms. Gradually the screw extended and gripped on to the beam. It pressed harder and harder into the wood, which splintered and cracked as the screw plate bit into it. The man, who was turning, grew exhausted with his effort and had to fall away. Another immediately took his place. Ice-cold water poured in upon him as he continued to turn the arms. As the screw bit deeper and deeper, he grew slower and slower but still he continued to pull round – to pull on the precious handles that raised the life-saving jack.

'Keep her moving! Keep her moving!' came the encouraging cries. 'She's going back! Keep her going, friend. Keep her going.' Yet another man had to take over.

'The water's easing! It's slowing! Keep her going.'

The beam groaned all the while. She groaned in resistance to the efforts to get her back. But the screw kept on turning and turning. Round and round. Bit by bit. Relentlessly the ever-lengthening screw pushed the beam back. The other end bit into the deck but the beam moved. She kept on moving – slowly, oh but so slowly – but move she did – slowly but surely. The deluge became a trickle. The trickle became a drop. At last, it was over. The beam was back. The screw gripped and held her back. The split was closed. The sea was kept out.

'One more turn – to make sure.'

'That's it! She's back! We're saved – we're saved,' came the rejoicing cries. 'Praise God for the jack-screw.'

The captain looked round the company. Every face was alight with relief. He, too, had a great smile across his lips. 'Yes – yes, we're saved. She'll hold. She'll be all right now. That was a piece of good luck, my friends.'

'No! No! Let that never be said,' replied Mr Lovelace. 'That was no luck, sir. That was the providence of our God.'

'I don't know about that.' The captain waved his arm and turned away. 'I don't know about such things.'

Mr Lovelace gripped his sleeve and pulled him round. 'But we do! It was God's goodness – else we should have been broken to pieces and ruined by now.'

16 *Turn Back!*

THE storm dragged on, unabated. Prudence found her eyes on several occasions return anxiously to the great screw which held the beam. How relieved she had been when some men had made the whole thing more secure. They had hammered in several mast wedges, long thin tapering pieces of wood, as tall as a man, to hold the mast in position. They had fetched a stout post from the hold below and forced it into position against the beam to make extra support for the vital weak part. She was glad to see the comfortingly strong ropes securely lash all in place. 'How good God has been to deliver us from such great danger,' she thought. She sighed, closed her eyes and leant back.

A certain measure of calm descended once more upon the storm-weary company. As the tempest dragged on, hours merged apathetically into days. Days merged into nights. The Pilgrims knew not whether it was day or night – nor did they care. Nothing changed below. Nothing. The vile smell of the airless hold, the cramped conditions, and the lurching of the *Mayflower* all played their part in the relentless sapping of the Pilgrim's strength. Blank, deep-set eyes peered out of their lined and leaden faces. The people were drained, haggard and aged. Death, welcome death, felt very near. All that was left in the world still in possession of life and vigour was the raging storm outside. As the ship dipped down, down into the ocean, it seemed to Prudence that they might never come up again. And who cared?

'Will we go right to the bottom? . . . Will we drown? . . .

What tangle of weed awaits us? . . . What fierce monsters lurk
below? . . . How far down is it to the bottom? . . . Will we
die in this wild, trackless ocean? . . . Have we come all this
way and suffered so much – just to die and be lost without
trace? . . . What will it be like to die in this cold, untamed
and surging sea?' Gnawing pain and fitful dreams were the
never-ending companions of the Pilgrims. Sickness, stench,
stale air . . . on and on, went the relentless torment.

'Attention, please. Can I have your attention, please?' The
captain had come into the hold. 'I need three of your number
to speak for you in a conference.' His powerful shout aroused
the people.

'What's the matter? What d'you want?'

'Please, my friends, it's important. Don't lose time, argu-
ing. Choose three who will speak for you – responsibly.
Please do as I ask.'

The Pilgrims hastily chose three of their men for the
captain's conference. They included Mr Lovelace. The three
joined the captain and soon had vanished below.

'What can it mean? I wonder what it can be?' whispered
Prudence to her brother.

Justice did not answer. Instead, he tugged his sister's arm
and put his mouth close to her ear. 'Follow me,' he whispered.
'Don't make a sound.' They crawled across the floor to the
steps and very cautiously made their way down the topmost
couple. They focused their attention on the group of men
who stood below. They saw their father, clutching on to a
beam to hold himself against the tossing of the ship. Likewise,
others were clinging to ropes or gripping the roof beams to
keep themselves steady. In addition to the captain and the
Pilgrims, there were three of the Adventurers and a couple of
the ship's officers. The children could just about distinguish
the sense of the animated conversation above the din of the
storm. The Pilgrims had a most resolute look on their faces.

'We will not turn back.' Mr Lovelace stated, simply. 'No!
We will not go back.'

The captain replied. 'My officers have had a ballot,' said he. 'Some of the men want to turn back. We must face the facts.' He enforced his arguments by plucking the fingers of his left hand with the first fingers of his right. 'Look – first – we've had a broken main beam. Second, we've lost a good bit of sail torn away in the wind, just ripped off. Gone for good. Next, the cordage is in a sorry state. Most of the rigging is broken. Some of the spars are gone. Down below, you've had nothing but continual sea-sickness for days. Day after day you've been near death's door. My men have had enough. They've had a free vote and – well – they want to go back. That's the position. You must face facts.'

'Never! Never! Never! We will not go back,' snapped Mr Lovelace in reply and raising his voice. 'We will not go back. We will not! Not we.'

The other Pilgrims added their voices to his. 'We've suffered most,' they said, calmly. 'We're land folk. We're not used to the sea. Down below we've not eaten for several days. Our children and women with us have had nothing but stench, sickness and tears for days on end. And nights. We've suffered the most. But! In spite of that we will not go back. We will not go back. We will not.'

The captain slowly turned to face the Adventurers. 'What say you? What's your view?'

They were undecided. One said, 'Well, there's a case for and against.'

'There's no case for going back,' came the strong, stern reply from a Pilgrim. 'There's no case at all. I know we've all suffered but we've travelled safely thus far. Anyway, if we do go back we have no more hope of success than by going on. If we were to swing round, there's no certainty we should make landfall in time.' He addressed his final remark pointedly to the captain. 'There's no certainty, is there, captain?'

The captain slowly shook his head. 'No – no, of course not. I couldn't say for certain that we should be bound to make landfall in safety. No – no, I cannot promise anything,' he added, harshly.

'Well, it's madness even to think of such a thing, then. We committed our cause to God and he has preserved us so far – and he will keep us to the end,' said Mr Lovelace.

'Tchah! Stuff and nonsense,' spat out an Adventurer. 'Foolish talk! You religious people and your religion make me sick. Your religion makes you lose all sense. You're like women. You and your Bible quoting.'

'Strange. Strange, that is,' said Mr Lovelace calmly. 'Why, that is strange. You say we're like women and have women's strength and yet, we with women's strength want to go on – whilst you – with the so-called strength of men – want to turn back and run to England. Rich that is!'

'Well said, Matthew, well said.' A fellow Pilgrim voiced his approval. 'Well said, indeed!'

The ship's officers were put out at his remarks. The

Adventurers, too, had nothing to say in reply. The conference had reached stalemate.

'I will tell you what we shall do,' said Mr Lovelace with authority, taking command of the negotiations. 'Let's go above – to the hold. Let's ask the whole company of the Pilgrims for their opinions. After all, they've suffered most. Let them have their say. We give you our word that if they're for going back – so be it, we'll agree to turn round. On the other hand, if they will go on – let's hear no more of the foolish talk of turning round. Well men,' said he, looking round at the sailors and Adventurers, 'what say you? Do you agree? Do you agree? Speak!'

The Adventurers sullenly growled their approval. One spoke for them all. 'I suppose so.' They smarted still under the earlier rebuke.

The captain lifted his face. 'Well, it seems reasonable and fair to me. You have women and children with you. 'Tis true you have suffered even more greatly than we. What you propose is reasonable. Yes – let's go up and see what they say,' he concluded in a more cheery voice. He turned to his men. 'Do you agree, men? If the women and children want to go on, it should be easy work for experienced sailors, eh?'

'Quick! Quick!' whispered Justice to his sister. 'Back! Back! Quick!' They scrambled back to their place. Their mother was most puzzled to see their darting return. 'Where have you been?'

But before they could answer or, rather, before they had to answer, the men had come up from below.

'Attention! Listen my friends,' called our Mr Lovelace. Wondering eyes turned towards him. 'The captain has a proposal to put to you all. A serious proposal. Listen. Listen, my friends, to what he has to say. Think carefully about it. Make no hasty decision. And when you have thought about it – well, give us your opinion.'

The captain stood forward. He raised his voice. 'My

friends. You have suffered much. You have passed through many perils that must have been new and very strange to you.' A chorus of agreement sounded round the hold. He went on. 'I must tell you that we have suffered much loss in this storm. I must tell you the ship is in a dreadful and sorry state. You can see,' he said, pointing to the jack-screw, 'you can see some of the trouble down below. But up above it's no better. Sails are shredded to ribbons, spars are smashed and broken, sheets are gone. We're nothing less than a floating wreck. And that's the truth of it. Now. Now, some of my men are for turning back. I must be honest with you. We've had a parley.' He waved his arm vaguely at the small group behind him. 'Some don't know what to do. Some want to go on. And some want to turn back. We can't agree. So we've decided to put the matter to you. What you decide, my friends, will be the decision. So, what d'you say, my friends? What do *you* say? Go on or go back? What's it to be?'

The people were greatly taken aback. They were much perplexed. Hurried, puzzled glances were exchanged. 'Go back? Go back?'

John Howland broke the silence. He lay in the corner, still spasmodically coughing after his near drowning. He slowly and painfully raised himself upon his arm. With a feeble voice he spoke. 'God has kept us. He has kept us so far and especially has he kept me, though I so foolishly rebelled and sinned against him – and this whole company.' He had to stop. A fit of coughing came upon him. Everyone waited. Every eye was upon him. After a while he began to speak again. 'God will keep us through the rest of the voyage, I say. D'you think that God has delivered us from so many dangers to let us drown now? 'Twould be wrong to go back.'

Another stood forward. 'I agree. Let's go on. We're not the first like this. We're not the first to have this trouble. The Apostle Paul did so long ago. Remember, he was in such a strait as this. They didn't see sun or stars for many days and whilst the storm raged they, too, gave up all hope of deliverance. But I feel like he did and I agree with him. Let's keep our courage and have faith in God. For my part I say let's go on, let's go on – trusting in the Lord.'

A chorus of 'Amens' sounded from the Pilgrims at his remarks. 'Yes – that's right.' One or two even self-consciously clapped, briefly.

'What of your women?' said the captain. 'That's the voice of the menfolk. What of you – you mothers? What say you?'

Mrs Lovelace spoke up. 'I am with my husband,' she said calmly. 'Let's go on.'

'I am with my parents. Let's go on, please,' the weak, trembling voice of Prudence sounded. She listened to her own words with amazement. 'Can it really be me that is speaking? Me?' She tried very hard to sound brave, but she could not help showing her nervousness by her trembling voice.

'Well spoken, young mistress Lovelace.'

'Now, that's rich, that is. That's rich. I confess I never heard the like before,' admitted one of the officers. 'Out of the mouths of babes and sucklings, eh?'

'Come, my friends, you have heard the opinions of others. What do you say for yourselves? What say you?' said Mr Lovelace boldly. 'Do we go on – or do we go back? What's it to be?'

'Go on! Go on! Go on!' roared the multitude.

'Is there a voice against such an opinion?'

Silence reigned.

'For the last time – is there anyone for going back?' There was no reply.

'Thank you, my friends,' said Mr Lovelace quietly. 'Thank you.' He turned to the captain. 'There you are, sir. I think you have your answer.'

'We do indeed,' the captain replied. 'Let's hope that your confidence in God is not misplaced, my friends, that's all I can say. The ship's a floating wreck I tell you. We're miles and miles off course. I cannot tell where we are. I hope your confidence in God is well founded. That's all I can say.'

'It is sir, you can rest on that. But it's not our confidence in God that will keep us,' said Mr Lovelace to him. 'No – it's God, himself, we trust – not our confidence. He will keep us.'

17 *Relief at Last*

A T last! At long long last, the storm began to die. Justice and Prudence had long given up hope of seeing daylight ever again. Or walking, running or jumping in the fresh clear and warm air. 'Are we always to be in this cramped and airless hold? Shall we never be free from seasickness?' they thought many times.

But gradually the wind lessened. The waves no longer pounded the deck with such vehemence as before. True, the rain still beat upon the ship. But the storm had reached exhaustion point, like the passengers. It, too, had given up the struggle. The *Mayflower*, although appallingly battered, had come through. They had survived!

'We're through the worst,' comforted Mrs Lovelace. 'We shall come through. Lie still, just a bit longer.'

Excitement reigned! The longed for – and oft prayed for – words flashed through the hold, 'If the storm continues to die down at the present rate, the hatches will be opened within the hour.'

Each Pilgrim's spirit was lifted. 'Hatches – open – fresh air, again!' A gigantic load was taken from every heart. The Pilgrims were free to be human again. Free! God had delivered them. They could live again. They had been brought through! They had triumphed! God had delivered them.

At last, the hatches were removed. All who could, sought to go on deck – immediately. They queued, patiently, at the foot of the steps and meekly waited their turn to climb. Excited murmurs bubbled amongst them. They tried, but with only moderate success, to suppress their exhilaration as they waited for, and anticipated, fresh air, at last. It was hard work for the enfeebled Pilgrims to drag themselves up the steps. And – what a sight met their eyes when they did, eventually, step out on to the deck!

At first, they were dazzled by the brightness of the light. It overpowered them. Although the skies above them were still leaden, it was bright as a midsummer noonday to the near-blinded sufferers. As they gradually grew accustomed to the startling brightness, they were amazed at the extent of the damage before them. They had grown so used to hearing, in their din-battered ears, the violence of the tempest through which they had sailed. Now, they could see the effect by the state of the ship. Wood, everywhere, was splintered and smashed – smashed to smithereens. A ragged cloth – a mere apology for a sail – flapped and cracked at the mast. The ropes were being thrown about wildly in the wind. They writhed aimlessly.

The Pilgrims walked about, vaguely staring at the chaos around them. They could not believe that this – this – this shambles – was the same *Mayflower* that had left Plymouth. They could not take it in. Sailors were doing all they could to put the ship to rights. They had rigged up safety lines so that the passengers could get about by grasping the rope with two hands. The captain stalked around the ship with obvious purpose. He shouted his orders. His men sprang into life. They, too, were relieved to be up above once more. Spare sails – old and stained – were hastily dragged from below. New rigging was put together. Makeshift repairs went on all around.

'Come on, you lubbers, let's get her shipshape again. To work men. To work, with a will.'

Before long, the songs of the sailors announced the return of something like proper order to the *Mayflower*. The ship bent willingly to the moderating wind. She, too, was glad

she was under sound direction again. She was no longer at the mercy of the wild and unpredictable storm.

Justice and Prudence took it all in. They were enthralled. 'Let's go to our place – our special place.' Prudence had to yell to Justice to overcome the force of the wind which still possessed great power. She called to her brother and pointed forward. They pulled their way along the ropes very slowly and very carefully. And what a shambles met their eyes! What a mess! Instead of their cosy, orderly nook, they saw only a pile of broken spars and other bits of splintered wood. Water slopped about everywhere. The locker was split and wrenched from its moorings – its precious contents spewed over the deck. The place was a ruin. The children stood, surveying the scene – silent – stunned.

'Will it never be ours again?' cried Prudence, after a while and with anguish.

'Of course it will,' replied Justice, with far greater cheer in his voice than he felt in his heart. 'When the sailors can get round to tidy up the place and – and – when the sun shines again, it will be ours once more. You'll see.'

And so it was. Why! the very next afternoon Justice and Prudence were to be found, once again, in their special hide-away. The wind had now moderated to a gentle breeze. The sun shone upon them. The long, long days of seasickness, fear, sobbing and pain were almost forgotten. Almost! 'Will we ever be able to erase from our minds, the memory of those dreadful days and nights of enforced captivity in the dungeon below?' Prudence voiced her doubts.

'We shall have nothing more to fear now,' said Justice. 'The worst of the voyage is over. 'Twill be plain sailing, from now on.'

But how wrong he was! All unknown to him, another cause of great fear and sorrow was fast approaching their world of bliss. A far greater fear, much worse than they had known hitherto.

18 *William Butten Causes Trouble*

THINGS were soon restored to the normal level of hardship aboard the *Mayflower*. After the storm gave way, the usual movement of sailors in performance of their duties took place between decks. One morning, it happened that Justice and Prudence were, unusually for them, still below after most of the other passengers had gone above. Only John Howland was left with them, and he was lying in a corner. He was still very weak after his dreadful time in which he nearly drowned.

A young sailor, William Butten by name, came up from below. As he came into the hold, he caught sight of Mr Howland. He failed to notice the children as they lay quietly in their dark corner. William Butten paused. He gently scratched his cheek. A pleasant thought flitted across his mind. A sly grin came upon his lips. He slowly swaggered over to Mr Howland, and stood over him, an imposing giant. He kicked out at Mr Howland's legs.

'Not feeling so good today, Pilgrim, eh?' he challenged.

Mr Howland made no reply.

'D'you hear me? D'you hear me? Your God don't seem able to get you to rights, do he?'

Mr Howland still said nothing. He made no move. He kept his eyes riveted to the deck.

'Insolent Pilgrim! Speak! Can't you hear me, man? Where's your manners?'

Mr Howland slowly turned and lifted his head and – with obvious, great pain – raised himself on one arm. He slowly leant his weight against the boards and bent his ashen, drawn face upwards – upwards towards the grinning, sneering sailor. He looked into his leering face. He saw his thin weak lips, standing out smoothly against his stubbly chin. Mr Howland began to speak weakly, with breathless discomfort. 'My advice to you is that you should watch your words, sailor.' His words were lost in a bout of enforced coughing. 'Watch your words.'

'Watch my words! Watch my words! Why should I?' retorted William Butten. 'Look at me. Did you ever see such a fit young sailor, well, did you? And look at you – a coughing, spewing wreck of a man. Watch my words! Watch my words, indeed! Who are you a-speaking to, eh? Look you here, Pilgrim Howland, ain't it? Look at you – you say your prayers night and day – and you – wasting your hours a-reading that great Bible – just look at you. You're all the same – you Pilgrims. You've passed through a bit of a storm and you've all been sobbing and sickening everywhere. What good has your God done for you? You and your God! No time for him meself. I don't believe in him. I'll tell you what – I'll prove to you that there ain't no God.' William Butten paused, raised his voice and in mocking solemnity went on, 'If there's a God. If, I say, let him smite me down dead now – now, this very moment, I say.' He paused. Nothing happened. He roared with laughter. 'See there ain't no God – there ain't one, I tell you.' He leant down towards Mr Howland. He pushed his sneering face close to the sick man. He prodded him in the chest with his grimy nail-chipped finger. 'I'll give you something to dream about. Think of this, Howland. We'll bury you at sea yet, my friend,' he leered. 'You'll feed the fishes yet. And I'll tell you summat else. That's not all. How I shall laugh that day! Laugh? I'll laugh when we drops you over the side, that I will. You and your religion! I'll laugh – I'll laugh fair to split me sides – that I will.' With that, he burst into a haughty guffaw.

Mr Howland began to reason with him. 'Have you no fear of God?'

'God? God? Who's he? There ain't no God – saving meself,' came the sharp reply. 'Didn't I just prove to you that there ain't no God? Eh? Answer me that.'

'Have you no thought for your immortal soul?'

'Soul? What's that? Fairy tales – and what's more – I don't care about it – all I worry about is me liquor and me money. Spirits and ducats for me.'

'What about eternity?' went on Mr Howland. 'Have you no fear of death? Have you no fear of God's judgement? Have you no fear of hell? Don't you wish to get to heaven when you die?'

'Heaven and hell? Heaven and hell? I don't believe in such things,' he roared with a sneering laugh. 'I don't waste my time thinking about 'em. Die? I want to live. I want to live, I tell you. I want to live now.' He kicked out at Mr Howland again. 'You Bible preachers,' he called out, 'you don't know what life is.' He spat upon the floor. 'Keep your hell and judgement! Keep your heaven! Keep your Bible! Keep your soul! Immortal soul, indeed!'

He turned away. As he did so, out of the corner of his eye he caught sight of Justice and Prudence, huddled back in the shadow. They had drawn back in fear as they had listened to his blasphemy. They had drawn back as far as they could.

'Huh – huh, huh – huh.' Butten said slowly. 'What have we here?' Eh? What have we here? . . . spying Pilgrims, is it? Huh.' He strutted across to them. 'Little'uns! You there! Come out! Come out!' he commanded. 'Come out here, I say.'

He bent down to Justice, caught him by the hair and dragged him to his knees. Butten twisted the strand of hair, tugging, wrenching, all the while. Justice's eyes filled with water, overflowed and the salt stream gushed down his cheeks. He bit his lips to hold back his scream.

'You let my brother go!' howled Prudence. 'Let him go! Let

94

him go!' She sprang upon the sailor. All fear forgotten and caution cast to the winds, she hit him, flailing with her arms and fists. She kicked his legs, barked his shins and snatched at his greasy mane. She was like an untamed animal. Clawing, snapping, biting, pulling, beating and slapping. The tears freely flowed down her flushed cheeks. Tears she knew not that she shed. She shook all over with rage. 'Let – him – go. Let – him – go,' she screamed wildly. 'Let him go.'

'Get off me, you wretch. Get off.'

'Silence! Silence there!' The voice of Mr Lovelace rang out. 'What's all this? What's all this, I say?' He walked swiftly towards them. 'Stop it, Prudence,' he called out. 'That's no way to behave. Stop it! What's all this? Answer me. I demand an answer.'

Butten released his grip upon Justice. Prudence staggered to a halt and gradually slid to a dishevelled heap upon the floor at her father's feet. She looked up through her tear-filled eyes, her cheeks flushed a vivid red, her chest heaving and panting. She yelled at her father, gasping for breath – taking great gulps of air. 'This sailor – here – this sailor here – has been saying horrible things to us and about us – horrible things. He pulled Justice's hair. He made him cry.'

'You do not scream at me, my girl. Speak to me properly or not at all. Now, what is it? Quietly.'

Prudence took a great, deep breath. 'This man,' she said in a quiet, unsteady voice, making a huge effort to hold back her tears and pointing to Butten. 'This man – this man has been saying horrible things to us, horrible. He's been hurting us.'

'They've been spying on me,' snapped William Butten.

'No we haven't!'

'Yes, you have,' he retorted.

'Stop it! Stop it!' shouted Mr Lovelace. 'Silence, I say. This is no way to go on. What is the matter? What is it, I say? Will somebody tell me what is going on? Please.'

'He doesn't believe in God,' said Justice in a trembling voice. 'He's been saying dreadful things about God.'

'Don't you?' said Mr Lovelace gently turning toward William and placing his hand lightly upon his arm. 'Don't you believe in God? Is it true? Is it true that you have no faith in God?' he asked, softly.

'No! No! I have not,' snapped back William, snatching his arm away. 'No! I have not and keep your hands off me. It's no business of yours. Pilgrim poke nose! And what's more – I despise the whole lot of you – that I do.'

He turned away and made towards the steps. Mr Lovelace called out to him, 'Young man! A word with you, if I may.' He beckoned with his finger. 'A kindly, well-meant word, my friend – remember – that it is the fool who says that there is no God.'

'Oh! is it?' replied William. 'Oh! is it, Mr Knowall? Oh! is that so? Let me tell you something. You're the fools. You – not me. And let me give you something to sing about.' He marched back to Mr Lovelace. He pressed right up to him. Mr Lovelace kept his ground. Butten stuck out his chin. He almost spat out the words. 'Think about this, Mr Bible-preacher. Think about this. Do you know how many of your sort die on every voyage like this? Tell me that.' He did not pause for a response. 'Well, I'll tell you. We nearly always have to bury a good half of the likes of you, my friend. So pretty soon now we shall be throwing some of you overboard,' he went on with a sneer. 'And every time one of you goes over, I shall be there – I shall be there to laugh. I'll curse and swear at you, that day. And let me tell you some more – I'll tell you this – I shall be there to give you that last push. That last push.' He looked down at Justice and Prudence. He bent his head. He laughed in their faces. 'Think of that tonight, you little spies,' he jeered. 'Think of that in your dreams tonight.' He laughed again. He continued his derision as he lounged his way across to the steps, climbed them and disappeared out on deck. They could hear his scoffing laugh, failing in the distance, as he went back to his duty. It reached their ears and penetrated right to the bottom of their heart.

Mrs Lovelace silently appeared. 'Whatever was all that, my dear?' said she anxiously. She scurried across to them. She looked into her husband's stern set visage. She reached her hands down to her children. 'What's happened? What's the matter?' The children rose – very slowly. Tears filled their eyes – huge, burning tears. Lumps filled and hurt their throats. 'Why are the children crying? Why are they trembling so? What's happened? Whatever is wrong?'

The children buried their faces in their mother's flowing, comforting skirts. Their tears flooded out. They wept profusely and sobbed deeply. They shook violently.

'William Butten has been here – blaspheming. He's been cursing and tormenting the children,' said Mr Lovelace with a deep sigh, turning away.

'And Mr Howland too,' added Prudence. Her voice was lost in the muffling skirts. She raised her face clear of her mother's dress. 'He's been kicking him. He hurt Justice . . .'

'It's all right, my child. It's all right,' comforted her father. Prudence felt the strong steady rocklike comfort of her father's arms about her.

'What shall we do, Matthew? What shall we do?' said Mrs Lovelace, in a pleading voice.

'Do? Do?' replied her husband. 'I'll tell you what we shall *not* do. We shall not take revenge upon him. That is one thing we must not do. We know the Word of God. We must obey it.'

He let go of Prudence. He bent down and pulled up his great Bible. With a few quick thumbflicks he stood ready to read. 'Bless those who persecute you; bless and do not curse . . . Do not repay anyone evil for evil. Be careful to do what is right in the eyes of everybody. If it is possible, as far as it depends on you, live at peace with everyone. Do not take revenge, my friends, but leave room for God's wrath, for it is written: "It is mine to avenge, I will repay," says the LORD. On the contrary: "If your enemy is hungry, feed him; if he is thirsty, give him something to drink. In doing this, you will heap burning coals on his head." Do not be overcome by evil; but overcome evil with good.'

He snapped his Bible closed. 'There you are. That is our duty. You ask what we must do. That – that is what we must do.' He slapped his Bible. 'We must pray for him, my dears. Pray for him. You children – d'you hear? – if he curses you again, you must make sure you do not try to pay him back. The more he curses you, the more you must pray for his soul. The more he hurts you, the more you must show him your affection. Do not condemn him. Pity him.'

Prudence looked up at her father. She spoke very quietly. 'I shall find that very hard to do.'

'And so will I,' said Justice.

'My children! My children – if it is left to us and our own strength, we shall find it not only difficult, we shall find it impossible. To do this we must pray to God that he will give us his strength and his grace. Only in this way shall we be able to show affection to this young sailor.'

★   ★   ★

William Butten caused many hours of grief and suffering to the Pilgrims. He would strut his proud way through the hold, cursing the Pilgrims, laughing and mocking as he swaggered amongst them. He especially directed his vile attentions to any who showed signs of weakness and suffering by reason of the voyage. He singled them out as fitting objects of his cruel scorn.

'Rot your souls – as well as your bodies,' he would bellow. 'The devil take you all.'

Justice and Prudence were thoroughly afraid of him. Every footfall made them start. Every shadow held his terror and spoke of him. They dreaded being found by him when they were on their own. Then, at last, he caught them. He caught them – all alone.

One soft and sunny afternoon, when the children were happily settled in their special haunt, he came upon them. His shadow fell across them. They peered up. He stood, he positively towered above them – an evil, ugly giant – his legs wide apart and his hands upon his hips. His pimpled face was hard. He had a vicious look about his eyes.

'Ah! The Pilgrim spies, again, I see,' he said. 'All alone, eh? Where's your Bible, my dears?' said he in mocking voice. 'Doin' your readings, eh? Getting ready for heaven, is it?' he paused. 'Can you see that sea? I'll soon be throwing you down there. What d'you say to that, eh?'

The children were frightened out of their wits. They sat, frozen and alert. They drew in deep draughts of air through their noses, their mouths shut tight and their teeth clenched.

'Let me give you a piece of advice, a bit of friendly advice – like what your black-hatted, Bible-preaching father gave me the other day. You young'uns – don't you dare to come out at night – you never know how you might just lose your step and just – just fall overboard.' He laughed – a deep, hearty laugh. He went on, very quietly. 'Or something worse – something far, far worse.' With that he slipped a thin knife from a brown leather belt around his waist. It glistened in the sun as he waved it just in front of their faces. The children could smell the salt upon his tunic, he pressed so close to them. They drew back, instinctively. The blade of the knife flashed before their eyes. 'See that?' he said. 'See that?'

The children could hardly miss it. Their eyes were riveted to it. They followed its every movement with rapid, anxious glances.

'Sharp that is,' he hissed. 'Sharp – sharp enough to slit little livers and cut out little gizzards. Or maybe – just maybe, mind – who can tell? I'll run my little razor friend along your pretty throats.' He ran his filthy finger along Prudence's lily-white neck. 'Maybe – maybe. Ah! Ah! you might get to heaven a deal quicker than you ever bargained for!' He flung his head back and laughed, a deep, deep throaty roar. There was not an ounce of humour in it. The children saw nothing funny to laugh at. They shivered, right down to the stomach. Butten's pitiless smile held no laughter in it. Justice sensed his head going light. He forced his eyes away from Butten. His legs were shaking. His hands were clammy. His mouth was dry. He made himself swallow. Butten was no ordinary bully. Ordinary bullies said more than they would do. He said less than he meant – far less.

'Come on then. Ain't you going to speak? What's your answer?' Butten rasped.

The children kept their silence. Their hearts pounded away within them. Beating, thumping through their minds, they heard their father's voice. 'Do not repay anyone evil for evil. Do not be overcome by evil but overcome evil with good.'

'Lost your tongues have you?' went on Butten. 'Lost your tongues?' He grew impatient. 'Speak!' he rasped through tightened lips. 'Speak, I tell you. Speak or I'll – I'll lash you.' He turned, spied a coil of rope and quickly snatched it up. 'I warn you,' he said coldly, 'I warn you. Answer your betters or you'll feel this. You'll feel more than the lash of my tongue – you'll feel the end of this rope.'

Still Justice and Prudence kept their silence, their dry lips glued together. They wanted to scream but they could not force out the words through their heavy lips. They cowered back against the side of the ship. Their eyes darted quickly about them. But in vain – it was useless. There was no way of escape. They were trapped – snared – as frightened rabbits caught in a net. They were hemmed in behind by the lockers and Butten, himself, towered above and in front of them. The children went white – ghastly white. Their blood-drained faces looked up at Butten. There was no mercy in his eyes. They were entirely in his wicked hands. Trapped!

'What will it feel like?' The thought flashed through their minds. 'What will it feel like – to be lashed by that rope?'

They saw Butten's arm move. They closed their eyes. They cowered back. They swallowed, hard. They held their breath. Their pulse raced. They clenched their fists – their nails pressed into their palms – their fingers white. They prepared themselves to feel the burning lash across the face.

But! The lash never came.

'That will do.' Their father! Their father! They heard their father's strong and steady voice. Their father's voice! 'That – will – do.'

Oh! What a relief! They both breathed such heavy sighs. The air gushed out of their lungs all in a burst. Tears flooded down their faces. They looked up through watery eyes. Their father's hand had gripped the wrist of the sailor. They saw the whiteness of their father's knuckles as he held on tight. He shook and shook Butten's arm. The trial of strength lasted an age. But Mr Lovelace did not falter. He did not breathe. Slowly, oh so slowly Butten's arm began to fall. His grip weakened. At last, at last the rope clattered to the deck. Mr Lovelace thrust the sailor's arm back to his side. 'That will do – I say that will do.' The wind rushed out of his lungs and he gulped deep draughts of air.

Butten had a most bitter and spiteful look upon his face. If looks could kill! He rubbed his sore wrist. 'You'll pay for

101

this,' he snarled through clenched lips. 'You'll pay for this. You'll see. A curse upon you and all like you.'

He shook himself free. He slunk away. After he'd gone a few paces, he turned. He raised his arm and waved his fist at the children. 'You wait! You wait you, you . . . You'll pay for your father's deeds this day. I'll get my own back on you yet – you'll see. No man handles me like that. You'll pay – you'll answer – you see!'

19 *Terrifying Dreams*

THAT night, when he lay down to sleep, Justice could not get the vision of William Butten out of his mind. He just could not. William Butten was for ever raising his fist and pouring dire threats and curses upon him. He would come and press himself into his mind and nothing, nothing could keep him out. Justice tried. But to no avail. And when he fell into a sleep, he dreamed of him. There he was – towering over him, looming larger than life. Sinister. He assumed colossal even terrifying proportions in his mind. He dreamt of him, lashing him with the cord, whipping him – cursing God and laughing at him, as he did so. Justice winced, it was so real. Horrific doubts and fears chased each other in furious, hectic races around the inside of his head. They whirled around and around, tumbling madly in his mind. They made him feel sick inside. Then – they vanished – to give a momentary respite. But almost at once, they appeared again at the door of his mind and entered without so much as a knock, 'by your leave' or 'if you please'. He awoke with a start in a most dreadful sweat, his body trembling and his arms waving frantically, his teeth alternately clenched and chattering. He pulled his knees up to his chin. He was scared out of his wits. He still heard William Butten's raucous laugh in his ears. He still saw William Butten's leering grin in his mind's eye. Justice glanced furtively around him. There he was! William Butten was everywhere. He was in every flickering shadow, large and grotesque, brandishing his short, sharp knife. Justice put his hand to his throat, half expecting to find . . . well . . . he feared to imagine.

'It's all right, my child – it's all right – lie still.' The soothing soft-toned voice of his mother gently reasoned with him. 'It's all right,' she reassured him. 'It's all right.'

Justice felt her soft calming caress on his fevered brow and flushed face. A cool cloth gently mopped him. 'It's all right, my dear – lie still – lie still – lie still – you'll come to no harm here.'

He fell back with a sigh against his mother and lay quietly in her arms. Her flowing dress was a comfortable cool cushion to his weary head and bewildered mind. Her gentle hand stroked back his damp hair and caressed his sweaty brow. His head rose and fell with her regular deep breaths. She tucked the coarse blanket close about him. 'Go to sleep, my child. You're safe here.'

'I've been dreaming. I've been dreaming about – about William Butten. I'm frightened, Mother. I'm frightened. I'm frightened he'll hurt me. I'm frightened he'll catch me alone.' He sat up with a start. 'He'll do such terrible things to me. I know he will. I'm afraid.'

'I know, my dear – I know. But you're safe here. Go to sleep, my child. It's all right.' His mother gently pulled him back. She patted his shoulder. She held him close. She bent her head and quietly pressed her cool cheek against his face.

Justice closed his eyes but he could not go to sleep. He dared not go to sleep. He feared to go to sleep. He did not want to see the face of William Butten again. He did not want to see William Butten ever again. No! Not in reality nor in his dreams. He dreaded him. He dreaded his return. He dreaded his curses. It made his blood run cold to think of the rope and knife. Just to think of it brought him out in a cold sweat. Justice lay awake, his mind full of trouble and worry. He lay unable to sleep for fear. He lay there – against his mother – kept awake during the long, dragging, endless hours of the night.

But if only he had known. If only he had known . . . he had no cause for fear. No cause at all. He did not want to face William Butten again. No! Never again! Unknown to him, never again would he have to face William Butten. Already, all unknown to him, God had begun to deal with that man. 'Do not take revenge, my friends, but leave room for God's wrath . . . "It is mine to avenge; I will repay," says the LORD.' If only Justice had known – if only he could have seen William Butten now – he would have realized that he had seen the last of that cursing sailor. Never again would William Butten curse and torment the children. Never. Never again. He had torments – plenty of torments of his own to cope with. Now – and more to come.

20　The Vengeance of God

THAT very night, as Justice lay so disturbed in his sleep, William Butten also lay awake. He, too, was afraid. He, too, was in a great sweat. He lay tossing and turning – writhing in his hammock in the crew's quarters.

'What's the matter wi' ye?' came a gruff, questioning voice, muffled and sleepy. 'Keep still there.'

William Butten let out a great bellowing curse in reply. 'Can't anyone show a body some fellow-creature feeling? I'm sick. The gripe's got to me. It's so hot in here. I feel like an oven . . . Can't anybody get me a drink? I'm like a lemon squeezed dry. Drink, will ye? Drink, I say.'

'Be quiet, will ye? Stop yer noise,' cried another. 'Let's all sleep while we can – we've worked 'ard 'nuff for it all day. Butten! You ought to leave off yer licker – that's yer trouble. You're rottin' your innards with drink, man. And you're upsettin' our sleep. Quiet there.'

The fever of the young infidel grew worse by the hour. Dawn found him in a tremendous, lathering sweat. Beads of moisture stood upon his brow, gathered into drops and ran on to his pillow. His blankets lay wet upon him. He ached in all his limbs. Stabs of pain darted through his body which made him scream out at times. The anguish of his mind deranged him. He saw things – strange things – fearful things. He was violently sick. He shouted and raved in his torment. Again and again, his whole frame writhed in a spasm.

'What shall us do wi' 'im?' said one of his shipmates. 'How can we ease 'im?'

'Give'm some strong drink and put 'im out of 'is misery,' replied an old sailor, 'he – an' us, too.'

'Why don't we send for one of them religious Pilgrims?' cried another. 'P'raps they'll know a cure or summat.'

'But he's a'cursed 'em – 'aven't you 'eard 'im – you must 'ave 'eard 'im boasting, 'ere. 'Es openly abused 'em – you can 'ardly 'spect men who've been sworn at and who 'ave 'ad their littluns and womenfolk tormented so to come 'ere to 'elp 'im now.'

'Send for 'em – all the same. They can only refuse – an' they may come. Look 'ere – 'es in a dreadful state. 'Es a-goin' to die aforelong.'

'An' a good job too, if you asks me. 'Es nothing but a braggart. A drunken swab! Good riddance too, I say. The world 'ull be a far better place – without the likes of 'im.'

'No! Let's give'm a chance. I know 'ee don't deserve it – but let's send for a Pilgrim – come on – let's send.'

'You do's as you please. I'll have nothing to do with it. Le'im die, I say. But you do 'as you please – I'll 'ave no part in it.'

'Well, I'm goin' to see if one of 'em will come to 'elp.'

So it was that a message was sent to the Pilgrims.

Justice heard the frantic sailor as he talked to his father most apologetically. 'Sir! William Butten – you know 'im, I b'lieve – well 'ee's sick of summit awful – colic or gripe – a fever disease of a sort I've never seed afore.'

Justice took in his breath sharply and held it. 'William Butten! William Butten! That dreaded name. William Butten – grievously ill.'

The sailor was still talking. 'I must warn you – 'tis only right – it might be dang'rous for you to come along there. Mebbe 'tis something you can catch yerself – I dunno – but we're desperate back there. We've done all we can for 'im. Nuthin' 'as 'elped 'im. Nuthin'. There's no more that we can do. We're at the end of our tether and no mistake. Willee come along, sir, and try to 'elp 'im? Willee come, sir? 'Es in a great sweat. 'Es crazed. 'Es talking wild. I know 'es b'n a'cursing you, sir, but, well . . .'

Mr Lovelace cut him off. 'At once! I'll come at once. Of course I'll come.' said Mr Lovelace. He snatched up his Bible. 'Lead the way. Be quick, man.'

Justice lay back. 'William Butten violently ill – and with an unknown disease.' He could hear his father's voice ringing through his mind again. 'If your enemy is hungry, feed him; if he is thirsty, give him something to drink . . . Do not be overcome by evil; but overcome evil with good.'

Mr Lovelace reached the crew's quarters with all haste. Guttering candles lighted the dingy warren. 'Where is William Butten? Where . . .' The cramped space was filled with a swarm of gawping sailors. Butten was in danger of being buried alive in a seething cauldron of goggling onlookers.

'Back there! Back! Let me get to him. Back!'

The hubbub gradually died away. An invisible arm opened up a narrow, tentative alley and the way was partially cleared for Mr Lovelace to reach the delirious man. With much squeezing and pulling, Mr Lovelace made his way to the side of the young infidel. He placed his mouth close to Butten's ear. 'Can – you – hear – me?' he whispered, 'can – you – hear – me?'

Button's crusted lips moved, very slowly. But no words escaped. Mr Lovelace stood as erect as the low ceiling would allow. He faced the onlookers. They were a motley crew. He made such a stark contrast to them with his black and white clothes, clean shaven face and sharp, clear eyes. All around him were sailing men with bloodshot eyes and gaping wild mouths that displayed teeth blackened, broken or absent – matted hair that supplied weird, fiercesome crowns upon many heads. Several faces were scarred – livid white against a grimy brown countenance. Mr Lovelace addressed them. 'Back men. I implore you – back! Give this man some air.' He pointed to Butten. 'Will you starve a man of air?' With much

108

shuffling, shrugging and shrinking, space was made as the crowd drew back. 'Please! Please! Keep silent. I cannot hear his words. I cannot tell what he is saying.'

'Aye, silence afor'im,' commanded one, who seemed somewhat to be a leader of the wild, untamed mob. 'If I 'ears so much as one'ee even abreathin' – one of 'ee – that man'll have to answer to me – to me and my fist, I say.' He paused. He turned to Mr Lovelace. 'You carry on, sir. They'll be all right,' he said, tossing his thumb over his shoulder. 'They'll make no more trouble, sir. I'll see to that.'

Mr Lovelace looked at him, but said nothing. He bent to Butten again. 'Can you hear me? Can you hear me?'

William Butten twisted and turned upon his hammock. He shouted out in a delirious raving. 'Away! – Away, I say. Get away! Get away, all of 'ee. Leave me be. Leave me be, I say.'

Without looking up, Mr Lovelace called out to the spokesman. 'Have you any water left? Any good fresh drinking water?'

The sailor's face fell. 'None, sir, none,' he said quietly.

Another chimed in. 'Bleed 'im – a good bleedin' will do 'im a power of good. 'T 'as 'elped me afore now.'

'Gee 'im some physic. Some physic's what he needs,' sounded a voice from the back.

With that, William Butten disturbed again. 'Physic?' he said, in a faint far-away voice. 'Physic. Did I 'ear physic?' His voice grew firmer, stronger, louder. 'Physic!' he shouted. 'I'll have none of yer physic. Physic – away with it! Vile potions! Foul mixtures! Away with yer poison.'

'Poison? It's saved a good many like you from death – and the devil.'

'Ah and 'ow many 'as it killed? How many 'as it answered for? Tell me that.'

A murmured chorus of approval and agreement ran amongst the mob. 'Aye, ees right an' all. 'Tis foul, vile stuff – that physic.'

Butten opened his eyes. He looked around him vaguely.

After a while he managed to focus upon Mr Lovelace, but with obvious difficulty. He spoke slowly in level tone with a far-away voice. 'Lovelace – Lovelace, ain't it? Lovelace? What are you adoin' 'ere. Who called you 'ere? Who sent for 'ee? . . . Away with 'ee. Away with 'ee. I want none of your medicines. None of your potions for me . . . None of your preachings 'ere, neither. Leave me be. Leave me be, I tell 'ee. Away with you – away with all of you.' Butten waved his arm wildly at the crowd. The effort of his speech-making had exhausted him. He fell back upon his sodden pillows. He started to lose consciousness, once again.

Mr Lovelace placed a cold damp flannel about Butten's sweaty brow. He tried to make him as comfortable as conditions would allow. He loaded yet another blanket upon him. He tried to speak to him again, but still he got no sensible reply – just the ravings of delirium. Mr Lovelace fell upon his knees and clasped his hands over Butten's blanketed body. He lifted his head toward heaven, his eyes tightly closed. 'Have mercy upon this young man, O Lord. Have mercy upon him. Spare him, if it be your will. Spare him – please. Deliver him from this raging sickness. Above all, O God, pardon his soul. Forgive his sins for the sake of Christ. Apply the precious blood of Christ to him. By your Holy Spirit's power bring him to trust in Christ and so bring him to be at peace with you. Oh God – Oh God, if it is your will – have mercy upon him. Save his soul, O God. May he be a trophy of your saving grace. For Jesus Christ's sake. Amen and Amen.'

After concluding his prayer, Mr Lovelace continued to kneel in silence. An awesome silence. Eventually he slowly raised himself and stood up. He faced the silent, breathless crowd. 'Call me at once,' he said. 'Call me at once – if he becomes sensible. Do you hear me? I want to be told, at once.' He brushed aside the hushed mob – they melted before him – and reached the door. He paused. He turned. 'Remember, call me – call me, at once.'

The midday report showed no change for the better. The young man was still in his delirious torment. Mr Lovelace paced the hold, impatiently. At about four in the afternoon a sailor came running into the passenger's quarters. 'Mr Lovelace! Mr Lovelace!' he called out, breathlessly. 'William Butten wants to see you, sir. He's calling for you. Come sir! Come quickly. He's taken a turn for the worse, I fear.'

Mrs Lovelace spoke to her husband. She gently laid her hand upon his arm. 'Matthew, take care. I do hope he wants your forgiveness.'

'I hope for more than that, my dear,' replied Mr Lovelace. 'I hope he wants God's forgiveness.' Mr Lovelace lost no time. He marched directly to the crew's quarters. When he reached William Butten, he found him half-leaning up in his hammock. He was coughing, furiously and deeply. His drawn face was a ghastly white. A trickle of watery blood ran from the corner of his mouth. It was obvious that the furious fires of fever still raged within. His deep-set, black-rimmed eyes were frantic and wild. Mr Lovelace drew near. He opened his arms towards the sailor. He reached out to the young man. He gently addressed him. 'You called for me. Here I am. What can I do for you? Are you ready to face God, young man? You are dying – you are dying – you have only a short time to live. Make ready to face the Almighty, your Maker. Do you wish to know the way of forgiveness and salvation? Will you let me read to you from the Bible?'

William Butten pulled himself up still further, with much struggling, effort and coughing. He drew breath very deeply and began to speak. His voice took on a devilish cry. 'Forgiveness? Salvation? Take and keep 'em. I want none of 'em. A curse on you, Lovelace. A curse on you all. I seek no forgiveness. I've no faith in yer God. I've 'ad no time for 'im. I don't want you a Bible preachin' to me.' He raised his fist. 'I say, a curse on you all. Die? I die an unbeliever. A curse, a curse . . .' With that an awful scream escaped his lips. It was heard all over the ship. William Butten writhed in an

111

agonizing convulsion. He fell back with a great gasp. He lay
still.

Mr Lovelace immediately went to him. He placed his hand
upon Butten's heart. He stood motionless. He said nothing.
He bit his lip. His face grew dark. Slowly, he raised his hand
from the sailor's chest. He took hold of the blankets in his
two hands and slowly, gently folded it over the sailor's stare-
fixed, mask-like visage.

'He's dead. He's dead . . . This is a solemn thing we have
seen today. William Butten is with us no more. He is
dead,' he said quietly. He turned to the wide-eyed silent
crowd. 'We have seen this young man pass into eternity.'
Mr Lovelace paused. He looked into the staring, silent
crowd, his eyes piercing each one in turn. 'Let him be a
warning to you all.' With that he pressed through the
throng and was gone.

Later that day as evening shadows grew long, the whole
company of crew and passengers assembled on the main deck.
No one wished to speak or dared to speak. Justice and
Prudence stared at a mysterious, man-sized bundle as it lay –
lonely – in a tiny cleared space along the side of the ship.
Their eyes could not leave the magnetic bundle alone. It

transfixed them. 'That's the body of William Butten,' whispered Justice to his sister. 'He's all covered with a sheet.' They exchanged quick glances.

One of the Pilgrim Fathers stood forward. He opened his huge, well-worn leather Bible. He began to read with slow and serious voice. His words carried to all the assembly of the people. 'Listen to the words of God. "Do not be deceived; God cannot be mocked. A man reaps what he sows. The one who sows to please his flesh, from the flesh will reap destruction; the one who sows to please the Spirit, from the Spirit will reap eternal life".'

The Pilgrim closed his Bible. He faced the congregation. His eyes ran round the whole company. He gave a slight cough and began to address them. 'My friends, a most solemn business calls us here at this evening hour. We all know of the last days of the young sailor, William Butten. We need no reminder of his daily cursing and swearing among us. Truly, he was one who attempted to mock God. Truly, he has reaped what he sowed. This day, God has taken vengeance upon him. We have witnessed the just hand of God in what has taken place today. Let him be a solemn warning to us all. You who have not yet been brought to find peace with God – let this dreadful day serve to bring you to the Father. Come in faith through Jesus Christ, his Son. Come by the power of the Holy Spirit. Ask God for his mercy to pardon you for your sins. Remember, William Butten trampled underfoot the blood of Christ – and he has gone to answer for it.' Raising his arm, the preacher swept around the whole company, Pilgrims, sailors and Adventurers, 'I say to you all today, prepare to meet your God. Prepare to meet your God. Young and old – all of you – I say to you – prepare to meet your God.'

As the preacher concluded his sermon, the rigid body of William Butten, still covered in the sheet, was raised – with great care and without haste – was raised to the side of the ship. Justice and Prudence, along with all the others, gazed at it with wide open eyes and held breath as it was steadied by Pilgrim hands. It seemed to lie upon the side of the ship for ever. Then – it was gone – in an instant it had disappeared from view. It plunged steeply into the foaming sea with a great splash. It was lost in the ocean's depths. The children never saw William Butten again.

21 A Lesson in Navigation

SEPTEMBER had passed into October. Dragging October, at last, finally yielded to November. The conditions on board the *Mayflower* grew remorselessly worse and worse. The relieving days shortened. The long weary nights lengthened. Less and less time could be spent above. More and more time had to be spent in dark confinement below. The stale air below decks became ever more stale. The cramped passengers, even more cramped. They had grown so used to bending their necks in between decks that they wondered if they would ever be able to stand upright again. The dry biscuits had long since been reduced to a mere powder in the barrels – and that a foul breeding ground of weevils. The tough salt meat grew tougher and saltier. The Pilgrims all became sick, heartily sick of the continual heaving of the *Mayflower*. 'Will this voyage never end?' Voyage? It was an imprisonment – a nightmare – a dreadful, terrifying, nauseating, endless nightmare – on and on, without respite. Monotonous, wearisome, painful, inexorable . . . And day after day, the endless, unfriendly ocean. Remote and vast. The Pilgrims came to detest their bitter existence.

Would land never come into view? . . . Was it a limitless sea upon which they sailed? . . . Was there any America to be reached, after all? . . . Were they lost? Lost upon a trackless sea . . . Would they run short of food and perish in starvation? They knew that if another storm hit them, their condition was so pitiable, their strength so puny, they and the vessel surely must succumb, this time . . . Would it not be better to die? 'Oh! to end this miserable, wretched sameness, day after weary day, night after dreary night.'

One sharp-cold November morning, a withering, relentless wind was beating off the sea, and the children were wasting their hours on deck. It had grown far too cold to endure lessons in the open and they had long been abandoned, with much misgiving by Mrs Lovelace but with undisguised relief by the children. Thus it happened that the children were wasting their morning hours on deck. Their eyes were fixed towards the western horizon, lost in a vague dream. They were mummified. Blissfully unaware of his actions, Justice, absent-mindedly fingered a coiled rope.

Prudence it was, who was called back to the reality of their presence on the *Mayflower*. She sighed. 'Will it never end? Must we endure it for ever?' She sighed again.

Justice said nothing. He was still lost in his vague dream. Prudence looked back, around the weary, pathetic ship. Her eyes took in the confusion of tackling and the still damaged-scarred reminders of the tempestuous days past. Her eyes fell upon the captain as he strutted amongst his men, carrying out his routine inspections and encouraging the sailors to renewed efforts. He was a fine, full figure of a man. Portly, formidable and imposing. He amply and comfortably filled his handsome costume. Prudence thought that he must have been poured into his clothes, and 'stop' been called only just in time. Suddenly, an idea struck her. Impatience obtained the mastery. She just had to obey the impulse. She shook Justice. She rattled him to life.

'Let's – let's ask the captain – let's ask the captain.'

'Ask the captain? Ask the captain – what?' he replied sleepily and with just a tinge of irritability.

'Ask the captain? Why! How much longer we shall be, stupid.'

'What – what,' queried Justice, still dazed, growing increasingly impatient and only half aware of his sister's meaning. 'What? Ask the captain what?'

'Listen, will you. Don't get cross! Ask the captain how long it will be before we get to America, of course.'

'Leave it, Prudence, leave it, do.'

'No! Come on – let's ask.'

With forceful vigour, she dragged her brother back towards the captain, who was, by now, busily (and heatedly) engaged in conversation with one of his men.

'Come on, don't drag.'

'Leave it, Prudence. Forget it. Leave it.'

But Prudence was not so easily to be denied. She put her head down, clenched her teeth and pulled. To her surprise she looked up – there she was almost bumping into the awesome master of the *Mayflower*. She glanced up into his weather-tanned face with his fine, well-trimmed beard. Warm shining eyes answered her enquiring glance. Prudence felt relieved.

'Well well. A deputation is it?' brightly said the captain, a mischievous smile playing in his eyes. 'Complaints, eh? Let's be a-having of 'em.'

'Complaints? Oh no, sir. No, with respect, sir, it's nothing like that. It's um – it's um . . .,' she stammered in reply.

'Well – speak out – my dear. Speak out – let's hear what you have to say.' He dropped his voice, lowered his head and went on. 'I won't bite you, you know,' he confided. 'I won't have you – ah – flogged at the mast – not *very* hard – anyway.' He laughed aloud, pleased with his joke and slapped the children playfully about their shoulders. 'Come on now. Speak up.'

'Well sir, it's this. When will we be in America? How much longer have we got to stay at sea?'

'Tired of it, are you? Had enough of Mistress Atlantic, have you, eh? Can't say I blame you. Aye. My young friends you've had a hard time – I know – but, listen, here's some good news – let me tell you this – the worst is over for you – the worst is over – aye, we should see your new home very soon – very soon, now.'

The children grew excited at this.

117

'You're telling us the truth, aren't you? You aren't – well – just – just – saying it to cheer us up and fob us off, are you? Just so as we can put up with some more bad times – like what we have had?'

The captain smiled in reassurance. 'No, my young friends. No. You shall see your new home very soon. The worst is over for you – and for me to! And I think the *Mayflower* will be glad to get her anchors fixed once again. She's had a rough enough time of it.'

'How can you be so sure?' asked Justice. 'There's no marks out in this wide sea.' He waved vaguely at the ocean all around. 'How can you tell where we are?'

'No. That's true,' replied the captain, 'there are no marks but I know we are very near to land.'

'How can you tell?'

'Don't be so rude to the captain. Speak properly, Justice,' hushed Prudence.

Justice looked sheepish. 'I am sorry if I spoke rudely. I did not mean to.'

'Rude? No! Inquisitive, that's what you are. You've got a large healthy bump of curiosity, and that's good in a young-un like you.' The captain gave Justice an indulgent tap on the head. 'You'd like to know? You'd like to know how I can tell we're near to landfall? Right! Then I'll tell you. You see – there are two ways – two ways that I know that we are getting close to land.'

'Oh!' said Justice – by now he was thoroughly captivated. 'Please tell us.'

'Aye, my boy – I will. Come with me – you too,' he beckoned with his hand to Prudence, and stepped out towards his cabin. The children followed as eager hounds snapping at their master's heels.

In a few moments, they were all cosy within his cabin, the door closed behind them. All was peace and quiet except for the ever-present gentle murmur of the ship's timbers as they creaked and groaned in the surging sea. The brown – red

boarded room, though spacious and airy, was dominated by
a massive mahogany table placed in its centre. The low, early
winter sun peeped into the room, piercing the lattice in almost
horizontal shafts. Specks of lazy dust danced dreamily in the
beams of hazy light, falling gently and with no trace of hurry.
The watery light played upon a much-stained chart as it lay
pinned to the great table. There was a great deal of twinkling
of shiny brass and polished red mahogany about the room.
Pieces of strange, mysterious apparatus littered the walls. A
dusty shelf of thick and well-worn books propped up a corner.
It was a veritable cave full of wonder and mystery.

'Well – come in my friends. Right welcome you are to my
cabin.' The captain opened his arms and ushered them in.
'Now then, let's see – how can I tell where we are?' He reached
out and picked up a wonderful brass and wooden instrument.

It was circular in shape with a cross in its centre. Attached to the centre were movable arms. 'Do you know what this is, eh?'

The children made no reply. Their puzzled, quizzical looks told all.

'Thought not. Well it's an astrolabe – an astrolabe.'

'A what? An as-tro-labe? Whatever's that?'

'It's like this. By pointing it to the sun and moving these arms, like this, see, I can take what we call a "reading". Then,' he stepped over to his bookshelf and whipped out a volume, 'then, I look up this book of tables.' He tapped the book with his fingers. 'I look up the right table and then I can tell our latitude.'

'Our lat-ee-tude? What's that?' The children were mystified.

'You don't know what latitude is? I see. Ahhmm!'

'No sir,' the children replied meekly.

'Ah well. Latitude, let me see, now. Latitude tells me how far North or South we are. D'you see?'

'Yes sir.'

'But, if I'm going to get our position right – that's only one thing I need to know. I also need to know how far West we've travelled from England.'

'How do you do that?' said Justice, his interest thoroughly aroused.

'Well, I can tell how far West, we are, by working out our speed.'

'How do you do that?'

'I use the log and line,' the captain replied.

'Log and line?'

'Aye. We have a great heavy log with a rope tied to it. The rope is knotted along its length. These knots are spaced every seven fathoms. When we want to tell the speed, we drop the log over the side – it's a very heavy log so it doesn't move very much. It practically stays still – well that's what we allow for – and as we sail away from the log, the rope pays out, see? As

120

we do it, we use the sandglass to measure a certain time and we count the knots we have payed out on the rope in that time. Then, if our sums are good enough' – he laughed – 'we can work out how far we've travelled in that time. When we have those figures we work out the speed. That tells me how far we have travelled each day in our westward journey – that's the longitude. When I've got that worked out and found our latitude – with the astrolabe as I told you just now – I come in here to the charts. I draw the lines on my chart and I can see where we are. The latitude line, I draw East-West and the longitude line, North-South. Where they cross is where we are. D'you see?'

Justice thought for a moment.

'Yes but, sir,' he said slowly, 'that can't be very accurate.'

'Justice! Whatever do you mean?' said Prudence worried by her brother's impertinence. 'Justice you mustn't be rude to the captain.' She shook her brother's arm.

'No, Prudence,' her brother replied, 'I'm not being rude.'

'No, of course he's not. He's interested, aren't you, lad?'

'Yes, sir, I am – very interested.'

'What do you mean then – not accurate?'

'Well, sir, it's like this,' said Justice slowly. 'It seems to me,' he said, 'that during a storm we might get blown off course – well, we would do, wouldn't we? And in all those rough seas you might not be able to measure the speed – perhaps for days – and when the storm was all over you would just have to guess – guess – how far we'd gone in those days.'

'Quite right! You're quite right, lad, quite right. You put some of my leading seamen to shame, that you do.' He laughed and slapped his thigh. 'Let me tell you somethin' else. That's not the only trouble. Think of this. Even when we do measure the speed in the normal way, the log must move about in the sea – true, it is heavy but it must bob about a bit. F'r instance, what if there's tides and currents? The weight'll be thrown about and that'll mess up me readings all right, won't it? Aye. You're quite right. Aye. 'Tis a rough and

121

ready way. But, see, it's the best we've got. O' course that's where the skill of being a proper navigator comes into it. I have to make allowance for all this.' He drew himself upright at his last remarks.

'Where are we now?'

He beckoned to them. 'Come over to the chart and I'll show you.' He paused in front of the map and thought for a moment. The words came slowly. 'I reckon – I reckon – that we're not very far away from this position – this position – here.' With that, his finger pointed to a spot upon the chart.

The children stared at it in amazement. After a few moments, Justice spoke up. 'Why,' he said, 'we're very near to land, sir.'

'Aye, my boy. I said we were near to land.' A twinkle came to his eyes. 'But, do you know, I was sure of that even before I took the measurements. I said to you on deck that we're near to land – d'you remember? I knew that without any of this,' said he, pointing to his instruments and books of tables.

'How did you know that?' said Prudence, 'without the measurements, I mean?'

The captain said nothing in reply. Instead, he walked across to the door, opened it and stepped out on to the deck. He beckoned the children to join him. They scurried out on to the deck. 'That's how I know we're near to land,' he said with a throaty chuckle and pointing to the sky. 'That's how I know.'

The children raised their eyes. 'I don't see anything,' said Prudence.

'You do. You do,' the captain exclaimed. 'You see exactly the same as I do, but . . . you are not observing.' He gently chided her. 'Look again – and listen.'

'I can hear the creaking of the boards,' said Prudence.

'And . . . and the hiss of the sea,' added Justice.

'Aye,' prompted the captain, 'and what else?'

'And some gulls screaming.'

'Exactly!' said the captain. 'Exactly – gulls screaming.

Gulls! That's how I know we're near to land. Those birds you can see up there have come out to join us – to welcome us. Aye. We're near to land all right. We haven't had them with us all across the ocean, have we? No! So, I should say that we're within a few hours of sighting land – a few hours, I reckon.' He pointed up to the main mast. 'I shall have my men up there very soon. You keep your eyes peeled and your ears open. Your days at sea are nearly over.'

'Thank you, sir,' said Justice. 'Thank you very much for telling us all about it.'

'Not at all, not at all. If I judge rightly you could have a good future ahead of you – if you wish to go to sea, my lad.'

'Go to sea? I never want to see the sea again,' Justice replied with feeling. He never wanted to see the sea again. Never! He had come to dread it. He feared its power.

'Nor do I,' added Prudence. The voyage had satisfied a lifetime's curiosity about the sea for her.

'Oh! you'll think better of it when you've got your land legs back once more. And that'll be very soon now, I'm a-thinking. We're nearly there.'

22 *But, Where Are We?*

THE children hurried off to rejoin their parents, excited by the – oh – so welcome news that they would see land very soon. 'Land again. Land? Is it possible? Is it true?' Their excitement bubbled over. How eager they were to tell their parents – how pleased were they to hear it. Mr and Mrs Lovelace received the news with a pleasure almost equal to that of their children. All the passengers had grown voyage and *Mayflower* weary and they longed for the land. Longed for it with aching hearts. The news spread like wildfire amongst the Pilgrims and soon the whole company assembled on deck. They dropped all else and hurried to gain favoured vantage points. They gripped spars and clung on to ropes. Some dangled precariously over the edge to try to get the most advantageous station. Scores of longing eyes strained at the horizon. This was made difficult by the low winter sun and many hands were raised to shield peering eyes from its blinding power.

The captain was evidently much amused. A knowing smile played about his mouth and reached to his eyes. He strolled amiably amongst the animated crowd and spoke to several. 'You've a long wait, my friend – if you intend to stay where you are . . . I shouldn't lean out *quite* so far, if I were you . . . Don't climb up too high, will you?'

But his counsel fell upon deaf ears. No one gave up his position. No one moved. Each one wanted to be the first to see the land. They had waited many, many days – weeks – for this moment and no one was going to rob them now. They

124

would savour this precious prospect – no one would deny them.

Mr Lovelace glanced down at Justice. He smiled. 'You're very quiet and thoughtful, my son. Is there anything wrong? Feel unwell, eh? Excited, eh? Too much for you, is it?'

'No Father,' replied Justice slowly, raising his head. 'No – no, there's nothing wrong – nothing wrong, exactly . . .' His voice trailed off. He fell back into his thoughts.

'But – there is something wrong. What is it, my son, tell me,' Mr Lovelace said gently. He bent down so that their faces were close together. 'What is it? What's wrong?'

Justice paused. He fought an inward battle. 'Well,' he said after a time. 'Well – it may be nothing – but . . .'

'Yes, my son. What is it?'

'Well, on the chart, I noticed that – I noticed that . . .'

'Yes. Come on. You noticed what?'

'I saw that we were a long way from Virginia.' The words tumbled out in a rush.

'Steady, my son, steady.' Mr Lovelace placed his hand upon his son's shoulder.

'We were a long way from Virginia. The captain pointed to a spot on the chart much further North than Virginia. Father, I don't think we're going to Virginia, after all. We're off course . . . and the captain knows it.'

'No, my son. No.' Mr Lovelace gave a faint laugh. He gently shook his head. 'You must have misunderstood. You've got it wrong. The captain is well aware that we're going to Virginia – and if he knows we've been blown off course by the storms and we've been taken too far North, he would have altered course long ago – long ago – to bring us to a more southerly line. No. You forget it. You must have made a mistake. Charts are complicated things. Much too complicated for the likes of you and me.'

Justice opened his mouth to protest. But he thought better of it. Slowly he closed his lips together. 'Yes – that's it. I must have been mistaken,' he thought. 'But – no – I am

125

right,' he went on in his thoughts, 'I am right. The captain *did* point to a position too far to the North – I'm sure we're not going to Virginia.' Anxious thoughts tumbled through his mind. 'What shall I do? What should I do?' His mind was greatly occupied with his problem, until, with relief, it dawned on him that all would be known very soon. There was no need to make a fool of himself. 'We shall soon know if it's Virginia that's coming up over the horizon. If I'm wrong, then no harm will have been done. If I'm right, all will know it.'

Justice turned his eyes to the West. All that was before them was the flat, open expanse of the endless ocean. The same ocean that had been their home for so long. There was no land in sight – none at all – but he knew that somewhere – somewhere – over the edge of the horizon their new home was fast approaching. Their new home – wherever it was. Whatever it was.

'Land ahead! Land ahead!' The strident voice of the sailor up the main mast rang out over the ship. 'Land ahead! Land ahead!'

The Pilgrims broke into a huge crescendo of cheers. The swelling sound reached a peak and fell. Then it rose again. The passengers gave vent to their relief. Down on the deck they were unable to see the land as yet – but the man aloft *had* seen it. That was good enough to be going on with. Now every eye strained to get a glimpse of their new home.

'I see it! I see it! There it is!'

'No! No! You're wrong! It's just a cloud,' said a scorning bystander.

'There 'tis! There it is!'

'Is that it? Is it?' Gradually Mr Lovelace was just able to make out a thin wisp – a faint grey line – a mere smudge – barely above the horizon. He lifted Prudence to sit on his shoulders. 'Can you see it, my child? Can you see it?' he said with an undisguised thrill in his voice.

126

'Yes – I think I can, Father. I think I can.' Her feet kicked, excitedly.

'Lift me up please, Father,' said Justice anxiously. He feared he would be left out of the pleasurable goings on.

Mr Lovelace gently placed Prudence back on to the deck. Then with his strong arms he lifted Justice to his shoulders. 'My – you are getting a weight,' he said. 'I won't be able to do this much more. Do you see the land, my son?'

'Yes. Yes I do. I see it, Father! I see it!'

Justice could hardly contain his excitement. He jumped up and down when his father put him back on to the deck. They stood on tip-toe and continued to peer into the distance. They eagerly scanned the fast-nearing horizon. Mr Lovelace placed one arm about his wife's shoulders and clung on to a rope with his free hand. Bit by bit, the details of the coast ahead became more distinct. As they drew nearer, they were able to see the surf pounding upon the shore. The whiteness of the breakers shone out against the grey-green of the land and sea. Nearer and nearer came the land. Slowly – oh so slowly! The children heard the increasing roar of the surf as the breaking waves pounded the shore. They spied the grim tangle of dark, forbidding woods, rising just beyond the shoreline. The whole was caught in a patch of thin watery sun.

'So – this is our new home,' thought Justice. 'This is it. This! Have we travelled the vast ocean – this dreadful nightmare of an existence – for this? For such a place as this?' Nothing moved upon the dismal shore – only the remorseless rolling surf. The children's eyes scanned the rugged, stark coast for as far as they could see. The sinister place was featureless – inhospitable – severe – barren. They scrutinized the miserable, forlorn strand. It was empty. A waste land. 'This – this – is our new home!' The speechless passengers stood, covered in gloom – a fitting accompaniment to the eerie, haunting silence around and before them – a silence disturbed only by relentless crashing of breakers upon the shore.

127

'This is not Virginia!' Mr Lovelace's voice burst in upon their dejected thoughts. But what he said only added to their gloom. 'This – this is not Virginia!'

23 *The* Mayflower *Compact*

THE Pilgrims gazed at the mysterious land which loomed before them. 'There's something wrong here. Something's amiss. I don't think that this can be Virginia,' said Mr Lovelace, sternly, to his wife. 'I am sure that this is not Virginia. Wherever it is – it's not the place we agreed to sail to.' He turned to a fellow Pilgrim standing beside him. 'Man,' he said, 'I'm sure this is not Virginia.' He pointed to the shore. 'There's something strange here.' Mr Lovelace tapped his son on the shoulder. 'I am sorry, Justice. You were right about the captain. It seems as though you were right. He did indicate a position on the map too far North. That's not Virginia.' He flung his hand, defiantly, towards the shore. A subdued but anxious murmur broke out from the bystanders.

Mr Lovelace moved off quickly and quickly gathered two other Pilgrims and sought out the captain. Justice and Prudence turned to see their father. They caught sight of him and the other two Pilgrims as they talked with the captain. There was a great deal of agitation. Mr Lovelace pointed to the shore. The captain shrugged his shoulders and the group disappeared inside his cabin. Almost at once, three of the Adventurers climbed the steps and vanished inside. Justice and Prudence wondered whatever could be going on inside the cabin. They could picture, in their mind's eye, the panelled walls. They visualized the chart upon the table, the captain seated before it in all his finery, the Pilgrims, dressed in black – Adventurers, stood around, their swords hanging from

129

their waistbelts. 'What can be going on? What can be going on?'

Without warning, the cabin door opened and out stepped the Pilgrims. How grim they looked, straight-faced and thoughtful! Their feet clattered down the steps and across the deck back to the Pilgrim company. Mr Lovelace raised his hand and appealed for silence.

'Order please, my friends,' he called out. 'Listen, please.'

The hubbub died down. Like a tidal wave, the noise receded until just one or two rippling voices could be heard. With embarrassment, these quite quickly ceased and silence descended upon the whole company. All that trespassed upon the silence were the ship's creaking timbers and the wild pounding of the surf upon the nearby shore. Mr Lovelace's steady voice carried loud and clear to the people. 'My friends – my friends. I am sorry to say that we have been deceived – yes, deceived – deceived yet once again.' He slowly shook his head.

A chorus of groans greeted his remarks. 'Are you sure, Matthew? What do you mean? Deceived?' Earnest cries escaped from a dozen mouths.

Mr Lovelace raised his hand to silence the disbelieving hearers.

'Yes, my friends, we have been deceived once more.'

'Are you sure, Matthew? Are you sure?'

'Yes, we are sure. I'm afraid we've been deceived once again. This is not the end of our journey.' He pointed to the shore. 'This is not our promised home. This is not Virginia. We are three hundred miles too far North.'

Another, louder chorus of despair sounded from the people. 'Three hundred miles – three hundred miles North? Why? Why, Matthew? Isn't this Virginia?' A forest of arms waved at the shore.

'No, this is not Virginia. I'm sorry to have to say this. I am afraid the Adventurers have made friends with the Captain – behind our backs. It's most likely they have bribed him to bring us to this place and not to Virginia. That seems – to us

– to be the most likely explanation.' He pointed to his two Pilgrim associates. 'As I said, we're three hundred miles too far to the North. This is Cape Cod, not Virginia. We have to swing to the South and sail down the coast if we are to reach our hoped-for home.'

'What's to be done, Matthew?'

'Listen my friends. We have decided upon two things. Listen. First, the captain will turn the vessel South and sail to Virginia – that was the contract – that is what we paid him for. We shall sail down the coast – keeping the land in sight – to reach the settlement. Secondly, we've decided we've had enough of being deceived. We've decided to draw up a covenant with the Adventurers.'

'What do you mean? What covenant?'

'We will draw up a covenant that we and the Adventurers must sign. A contract between us both. We've been deceived too many times. Well, we have, haven't we? We've had enough of lies, false promises and half truths. Remember, we've got to live with these people and set up home together. So we must know where we stand with them. And we want to know where we stand, now. So, we're going to arrange – and before we land, too – we're going to arrange that this new colony of ours shall be governed in a right and sensible way. We haven't sailed all this way – across the wild Atlantic – to lose our freedom at the eleventh hour. Do you agree, my friends?'

The Pilgrims nodded their assent. 'We do. We do agree,' said one for them all. A chorus of agreement sounded after him. The Pilgrims were weary with their journey – heartily weary – and gravely, bitterly disappointed at this latest setback. But – they were determined – determined that they would sail on until they reached their desired haven. And they wanted things sorted out before they set foot on shore.

'No one shall be allowed to leave the ship until this matter is finished to our satisfaction,' went on Matthew Lovelace. 'No! We'll go below now, with the leaders of the Adventurers, to draw up the contract. Then we shall have it signed and sealed. Not before that will anyone be allowed to leave the vessel.'

Without another word, the group of Pilgrim Fathers, who had so recently come from the captain's cabin, went below to prepare the document for signature.

Meanwhile, the captain gave his orders to swing the ship to the South. He vented his ill feeling upon his unfortunate men. 'Make more sail there! Make more sail there, you oafs and lubbers. Look lively. Move! Move!' The *Mayflower* groaned with this change of course. She, too, had wished for rest. She had longed for respite. The wind regathered in her sails. The canvas billowed. Once again she strained and she was forced to pull her way through the troublous sea. She started her run down the inhospitable coast towards Virginia in the South.

*　　*　　*

An eternity passed. Or so it seemed. It was, in fact, just a mere few hours – and the Pilgrim Fathers came up once again from below. One of them had some leaves of paper, fluttering in his hand. The paper was covered with much close, fine writing. The rest of the Pilgrims gathered inquisitively about him.

'Listen my friends,' Mr Lovelace said, 'we have drawn up the covenant as we promised. This is what we will do. We will read it to you now and if you agree with it, then all the heads of the families will put their signature to it. And so will the Adventurers. We shall keep our copies and it shall be the agreed law of our new Colony. Listen carefully. Listen carefully as it is read over to you.'

The man who held the papers stood forward, lifted them up, cleared his throat, and started to read. '*In the name of God. Amen. WE, having undertaken for the glory of God, and the advancement of the Christian Faith, a voyage to plant the first Colony in the Northern parts of Virginia, do by these presents solemnly and mutually in the presence of God and of one another,*

covenant and combine ourselves together into a civil body politic, for our better ordering and preservation.'

Justice and Prudence could not take it in. They could make neither head nor tail of it. 'What did it all mean, body – politic – what was that? Civil body politic? What did it all mean?'

Meanwhile, the reader was going on – and on. The children stole furtive glances around them. All the people had set, solemn faces. The man's voice reading the document droned on and on. All of a sudden – silence. He had stopped reading! He had finished!

Mr Lovelace spoke. 'You have heard the covenant, my friends. This is the contract we have drawn up with the Adventurers. If you agree, this will be the basis of our new Colony. It is up to you, my friends. Do you agree? Let's have your opinion. Do you agree?'

'Yes! Yes we do agree. We agree.'

'Are there any against?'

Silence. All heads glanced about them.

'Any against?'

Silence.

'Right! That's good. Let's get it signed – signed at once.'

They marched to the captain's cabin. One by one, the Pilgrim Fathers filed past the great table and signed the contract. The head of each family signed for his household. Then, it was the turn of the Adventurers. Their leaders added their signatures. In a very short time, the *Mayflower* Compact had been signed and settled. Both parties took their copies. The Pilgrims had had enough. Their minds were made up. They would be deceived no more.

24 *The Providence of God*

A LL the while, the *Mayflower*, blissfully unaware of the controversy she bore, sluggishly blundered on in her southward course. The Pilgrims were sadly disappointed to have to continue to sail in her. It was a grievous blow that caused many a heartfelt pang. How awful it was to turn away from the land! How it hurt! What frustration! How despondent they were! They had grown so weary with the voyage and their gladsome anticipation of landfall had been so rudely and so quickly dashed. They were just plain and simple folk, honest and open. Harm and deception never entered their heads, but – here they were – cheated once again! It had been a mortal distress – it shocked and offended them – to realize that they had been so badly treated. It left them numb inside. Vague, gloomy, listless. They were a bewildered company, sadly dazed and dejected. A blank cloud hung over them. They stood about the deck of the *Mayflower* – small desultory groups, mumbling to each other in apathetic low tones. Mumbling about nothing in particular. Mumbling to no one in particular. No one listened. No one bothered. No one cared. An air of languid dejection, mingled with confusion, covered them all.

The agony of their wretched circumstances pressed itself relentlessly into their minds. They could see the land – so near and yet so far. They could almost reach out and touch it – almost. There it was – so close. They looked with longing eyes and heavy hearts towards the coast. 'Oh to be ashore and leave this – this miserable, stinking *Mayflower* – for good and all. Oh to be rid of this squalid existence.' Yet they knew they must not yield to the temptation to put ashore – even for a short time. That would be fatal and they knew it. They had to go on. They just had to. They just had to endure their sad plight for a while longer. A few weary hours went by. They dragged – oh so slowly. 'Surely, someone must have made a mistake with the sandglass! Surely, we've been going South longer than *that* . . .' Even the vessel had given up hope. She had given up all heart for the voyage – she limped along, wearily. She dragged herself through the bitter sea.

The voice of the lookout broke into the sullen depression. 'Ahead. Ahead!' he screamed. 'Ahead! Look ahead!'

'What is it? What is it?'

The Pilgrims shook themselves. They came alive. Eager eyes flickered with concern. 'What is it? What is it?'

'Ahead! Ahead!'

Everyone ran to the bows, pressed forward and strained their eyes ahead. 'What is it? What is it?'

Justice and Prudence were held tightly against the side – crushed so they could hardly breathe.

'Ahead! Ahead!'

'What is it?' What is it?'

Ahead, they could see the flat sea – that was all. But – no – there – there it was broken – broken into a thousand frothy-white peaks. 'Waves! Waves – breaking right out in the open sea,' exclaimed Justice. 'There, look! There, look!' He tugged out his tightly-squeezed arm from between his pressed body and the side of the ship. He pointed ahead.

'What is it? What is it?'

As far as the eye could see, the ocean was alive – teeming – bubbling with white horses. It was a boiling cauldron, leaping, dancing, frothing and foaming. The Pilgrims could hear the crashing din of the huge breakers and the pulsating roar of the wild surf. Right out in the open sea!

'What is it? What is it? What can it be?'

A sailor's voice sounded behind them, falteringly. 'Dangerous shoals. It's dangerous shoals. That's what it is, all right. This is a treacherous place, right enough. We'd better keep clear of 'em. If we get into that – we shall be done for, that we will.'

'What will happen, sir?' Justice turned his head, anxiously peering up and back at the speaker.

'Happen, young Lovelace? Why – we shall be broken up – that's what. Broken up. It'll be the end of the *Mayflower*. She'll never stand that,' he ended knowingly, but depressingly.

'All of us too – I reckon,' added another.

Abrupt, frantic, unintelligible orders rang out from the captain. 'Look lively, there.' The agile sailors sprang wildly to their stations. With swift, short jerks, sheets were rapidly lengthened or shortened. Sails were altered like the wind. The helm was forcibly swung about. The ship was flung violently on to a desperate course of hoped-for safety. The sudden drastic alteration of the *Mayflower*'s course sent the Pilgrims tumbling about the deck. Many were flung down. Arms and legs went everywhere. Elbows were bruised. Knees scraped. Confusion reigned. Women cried. Children whimpered. Blood flowed from many a wound.

Justice and Prudence picked themselves up. Fortunately, they were unscathed – merely winded. They peered, uneasily, over the side of the ship. 'What will greet us?' The breakers were still there! Still there! Ahead of them. The ship was still ever shortening the distance between them and – and death! The wind in her sails attempted to drive the *Mayflower* to safety but still the danger drew her to destruction. The roar of the surf shut out all other sound. The waves tossed themselves in a frantic maelstrom. So close – oh so close. 'Will she hold off? Will she get clear?' The laughing shoals of death continued to send out their siren call.

But the faithful *Mayflower* resisted. She held her own. At first, oh how painfully, how slowly she resisted. But, she kept her distance and then, bit by bit – agonizingly slowly – tiny bit by tiny bit, she drew away. She drew away from danger and death. She had swung about. She moved off to safety. She was free! They were delivered! They were safe!

Justice and Prudence gasped with relief. They released their pent-up emotions and held breath. 'Safe. We're safe.' They were reprieved.

At first, the people were delighted to stand clear of the danger. But it rapidly dawned upon them, that these shoals were a real hindrance to their continued progress southward. 'What will it mean?'

'Mean? Delays! The captain is of the opinion that we shall have to put out to sea again so that he can bring us round behind the danger.'

'Put back to sea? Put back to sea? We're thoroughly sick of the sea.' The sea – the detestable sea. The Pilgrims hated the very thought of going back out to sea. Hated it.

'No!' A man stood forward and claimed the crowd's attention. 'Friends, listen to me. We've had enough of this ocean, have we not?'

'Yes.' The people gave a hearty endorsement to the sentiment. 'Yes. You're right, man. We've had enough of the sea. More than enough.'

'That's all very well, my friend,' responded Mr Lovelace holding out his hand, palm upturned. 'We can all agree to that. That's easily said. But we must be practical. What's to be done? What shall we do about these?' He pointed out to the frothy barrier. 'We can't get through shoals and reefs. It'll be sheer folly to try – plain madness. It'll be the end of the vessel – and the end of us too. We must face the facts. We must be sensible. There is no other way to reach Virginia but to go out to the open sea and round. Surely you can see that?'

His argument effectively silenced the people. They just had to face the stubborn facts that stared them plainly in the face. Wishing was not enough – that would not get rid of the foaming wall! They had to go out to sea to avoid the danger – if they were to reach Virginia.

A man from the crowd voiced an opinion felt in many a heart. 'The captain should never have brought us this far north. It's all his fault. We should never have been here in the first place.'

At this an old Pilgrim stood – or rather stooped – forward. 'Dear friends, listen to me,' he said, slowly, in his crackly, whistly voice. 'Will you listen to an old, feeble man? I feel rather like Jacob, today . . . You remember that Laban deceived and cheated him – cheated him over and over again. Yes . . . Yes . . . Well – but do you remember this? Do you remember what Jacob said about it all? Eh? Let me remind you of what he said about it . . . He said that in spite of the fact that Laban had cheated him, God had not allowed Laban to harm him. Now isn't that a very wonderful view to take of it all, my friends? God had been in control. God had his purpose in it. Now, I say I feel like Jacob. We've been cheated. Yes . . . that's true. Cheated badly . . . And that man'll have to answer for it. And we can leave that to the Lord. But this is what I say – God is in control. Might it not be his purpose to have us make landfall, back up north a bit? Eh? Let's be like Joseph – he was just such another as Jacob. Can't we say with him, that though the captain and these – these Adventurers – meant it for our harm, God meant it for our good? Eh? I know we didn't mean to make land at that point on the coast, but in the providence of God, that's what has happened. Now we're running into more danger. What I say is this. Can't we look upon it as guidance from the Lord? Let's go back – back to the bay we saw land first of all. Let's make our landfall there.' He stepped back. He was astounded to hear himself make such a speech. 'That's all. That's all I have to say,' he murmured apologetically.

The throng was silenced by his remarks. 'Can it be of the Lord? Is he guiding us, in this way? Is he stopping us now and telling us to go back north? What should we do?' One stood forward. 'I, for one, agree with our brother. Let's recognize the hand of our sovereign God in it. Let's go back.'

A muffled murmur of approval greeted his words.

'Can you do no better than that, friends?' he went on. Let's have better than that. We've had enough of the sea, haven't we? Yes! You know we have. Now the Lord has stopped up our way – surely it's his call to us to go back? Let's fall in with this clear and plain guidance from God. Let's go back.'

This time the agreement was heartfelt and full.

'Well, friends,' said Mr Lovelace, 'is that your opinion? Go back is it?'

'It is. Yes.' The words came from all quarters.

'Very well then.'

'What's this? What's this?' The captain appeared at Mr Lovelace's shoulder. 'What's this? Turn back?'

'Yes, sir. We've decided to turn back. We can see the hand of God in all this. We yield to his providence.'

'I'm heartily relieved to hear it, my friends. A wise decision – very wise if I might be so bold. We'll go about then. We'll be back at Cape Cod the morning after tomorrow.' He glanced across to a group of Adventurers. 'Cape Cod it is, then.'

25 Cape Cod

CAPE Cod came up over the horizon, for the second time. It was much harder to distinguish the land now. A snow flurry had started. At times, it thickened and blanketed the land entirely from view. Then it would ease and the drab land timidly poked through again. The Pilgrims saw and heard the breaking sea still pulverizing the shoreline. A pale, watery sun, out of a pinky sky, low and weak, played feebly upon the lonely, cheerless land. It was a bleak, windswept place. The powerless shafts of light pencilled the shore. There was little welcome here.

Prudence shivered in the biting cold. The cutting wind blew bitterly off the freezing sea. Her mother left her side and without a word, disappeared below. When she returned she brought with her two of the coarse blankets. She wrapped them about her children. Billows of steamy vapour puffed out of their mouths and hung about them in a dense clinging mist. Thin, hoary white spiders rapidly spread over their clothes. Moisture drops upon their blankets glistened frost-white. Rime formed on their eyebrows. The cold stung at the back of their noses. It forced them to sneeze. Their eyes smarted, reddened and ran. The frosty air punched their lungs. Their chests grew tight and breathing was an effort.

The sailors, awaiting further instructions huddled together and blew upon their frosted fingers, seeking all the shelter they could find to escape the all-penetrating wind.

'Make way! Make way there! Make way!' The gruff voice

of the boatswain rasped out his orders. He pushed his way forward, melting a narrow passage through the frozen crowd.

Justice and Prudence picked out the sailor who was taking the soundings. He was precariously perched in his tiny barrel, lashed to the sides of the ship. He reminded them of a small bird in his nest. He held the dripping lead in his hand and a great coil of cord attached to it. He raised his arm and threw the weight out into the sea. It hit the water with a mighty splash. The cord paid out in rapid pursuit.

'Ten fathoms,' the leadsman called out in a monotonous tone.

He dragged in the lead. When he had recovered it, once again he threw it out into the sea. 'Nine fathoms.'

The captain shouted his commands. The *Mayflower* was slowly turned to bring her head into the icy wind. Round she came – sedately – queen like. 'Let her go! Let her go!'

The chains rattled and scrabbled madly across the deck. A tremendous splash followed at once. The anchor hit the sea. The voyage was ended.

A strange, subdued silence came upon the Pilgrims. They had arrived. Arrived? At last! It was over. All over. They could hardly believe it. Their dreadful voyage was over. They could not grasp it. They could not take it in. 'Over! Over! The voyage is over. We have reached our now home.' No more would they have to tolerate the intolerable. The appalling hardship of the wretched life at sea on this tiny prison-ship was over. Over for good and all. Justice and Prudence dared not speak. They could feel the silent solemnity as it hung over the people.

The Pilgrims instinctively gathered in the centre of the open deck. Steamy breath surrounded them, fog-like in the frozen air. Snow silently – gently – fell upon them and clung. In spite of the snow, slowly, one by one, the men began to remove their tall black hats. Mr Lovelace broke the silence. 'Let us give thanks,' he said in a steady voice, with only the merest semblance of a crack in it. The Pilgrims knelt upon the hard wooden deck. Flecks of snow pitched upon their bared heads and upon their clothes. Justice and Prudence knelt by their mother. Only Mr Lovelace remained standing. They heard his voice as he gave heartfelt thanks to God for his protection for them upon the voyage and their safe arrival. All the Pilgrims had come to long for the dry land. They had come to hate the continual movement of deck beneath their feet. The endless motion. They hated their vile conditions at sea. They longed to feel the solid and stable ground once again beneath them. Justice and Prudence felt the depth of emotion in their father's prayer. They knew that all the Pilgrims felt as they did.

'O God, we thank you – we thank you with all our hearts, that you have brought us safely to this place. You have

delivered us from tempest, hunger and many great dangers. We thank you that not one of your people has died whilst we have been upon this voyage. You have brought us safe across this vast and furious ocean. We pray that you will accept our heartfelt thanks. Now, we pray that you will bless the foundation of our new settlement. May it prove to be for your glory and for the good of the people. Once again, oh God, thanks be unto you – thanks – praisèd be your great name for your wonderful goodness towards us. You heard the prayers of your people and you have answered them. We thank you, O God, through Jesus Christ our Lord. Amen.'

The final 'Amen', sounded as with one voice. The whole company joined in. They were united in their thanksgiving to God for his mercies towards them.

Justice and Prudence opened their eyes and furtively looked around them. They saw the men start to don their hats and the people slowly pulling themselves to their feet. They were flicking off the snow that had silently gathered upon them. No one spoke. Soft tears flowed down many faces – not of sorrow – but of glad relief and true joy. The Pilgrims had finally reached the land of freedom. Their freedom!

26 Landfall – At Last!

IN no time all was movement aboard. The small boat was quickly dragged from the hold. Hasty preparations were made to send ashore a small party to explore the lie of the land. Everyone worked with a will. Infectious, happy laughter rang out. Laughter of joy and relief. There was much back slapping and excited, nervous chatter. Laughs came easily. The ship was alive with agitated, cheery prattle. Even the thickening snow could not dampen their spirits. They had arrived. The nightmare was over!

'Father,' said Justice. 'Father, may Prudence and I come with you? We should so like to come – wouldn't we, Prudence?' He gave his sister a nudge.

'Yes, Father. Yes, Father. Please! Please! We would. Please may we come?' She tugged at her father's sleeve. 'Please.'

Mr Lovelace turned to his wife. 'What d'you think, Martha?' A twinkle shone in his eye.

Mrs Lovelace had an answering twinkle in her eye. 'Well, if there's room – and if they promise to be good.'

Their father looked down at their upturned, pleading faces and smiled. He gently stroked their cheeks. 'Yes, my dears. Yes – I think there might just be room for two small bodies – if they are very good, of course.'

'We shall be good. We promise.'

When all was ready, the exploring party was called to the side of the ship. The children soon clambered down the rope ladder – very slippery in the frost – lost their frozen grip and fell into the bottom of the rowing boat as it bobbed on the sea. With some shuffling and careful movement, coupled with much playful banter from the others, they were soon safely installed at the stern of the little boat.

'Are we ready?'

'Aye.'

'Right then. Let's cast off.'

The sailors took up their oars and pushed against the side of the rock-like *Mayflower*. Off they lurched. The sailors engaged the oars in the rowlocks and soon were pulling with a hearty will towards the shore. None of the Pilgrims in the rowing boat said a word. Many had a cold musket barrel clasped in their hands. The children spied the thin muzzles protruding above the shoulders of the men sitting in front of them. They stuck up through the mist of frosty breath. They and the black hats made strange mysterious shapes in the gloom – shrouded in the fog. All that could be heard was the gentle regular dipping of the oar blades in the sea and the answering raucous squeal of the oars in the rowlocks. No one said a thing. A spirit of fearful anticipation had come over them.

'What dangers await us on the shore?'

It was not a time nor a place for comfort. The biting wind entered their very bones. The little company pulled their clothes tight around them and jerked up their collars, high about their necks. Falling snow pitched upon them, melted and ran down their backs. The metal of the boat and muskets burned ice-cold in their hands. They shivered and drew close – to seek every last morsel of mutual warmth. The blizzard drove the sharp snow into their eyes. They instinctively screwed them up in self-defence. The little boat was steadily pulled through the thick water. The children turned to look back at the *Mayflower*. They found it difficult to recognize what they saw. They could hardly believe that such a tiny ship as the one before them – that such a tiny ship had been their home for nine long and dangerous weeks. They saw the rest of the Pilgrims gathered at her side and leaning over, gazing out towards them. Many were slapping themselves to try to keep warm. They could see and hear the flapping, beating arms. Some were blowing on raw, chilblained hands. The children waved out. Hands were cupped to mouths and cheery greetings dreamily floated back in a hollow echo across the still water. The snow flurry thickened yet further. The spectral ship began to lose its sharpness. Now they could only dimly make her out. She was a mere phantom coming and going into the snow flurry. In the few moments the children spent looking backwards, the whole of the voyage passed before their eyes, once again. They saw the raging of the storms through which they had passed. They felt the tempest's terror. They heard the whining wind as it whistled and screamed through the rigging. Once again, they heard the creaking of the timbers. They smelt the stale, sickening stench below. Master Reynolds and William Butten appeared. Justice shivered. 'Are you very cold?' whispered Prudence.

'No. Not 'specially,' he replied faintly. 'Just thinking. Just thinking – of – William Butten.'

'That's strange,' said his sister, 'that's very strange. So was I – so was I.'

They turned their eyes from the *Mayflower* with relief. They looked towards the land. It came as a shock to them to see how close the land had drawn since they had turned away. It loomed before them. The dark, forbidding woods rose steeply just above the shoreline – all shrouded white in fresh-fallen snow. All looked dark within, sombre and menacing. 'What strange wild creatures live there, in those woods? Are there fierce, war-like savages living there? What will they be like? Will we need the muskets? Oh! what is waiting for us? What is waiting for us in this land? What unknown dangers are lurking there?'

The snow still fell – silently – dampening all sound. The children pulled their blankets tighter and tighter around their arms and shoulders. 'How cold it is! But, fearful thought, what hardships will we have to suffer in the long, long winter

ahead? It is snowing heavily now and yet it is only November.
How hard life will be. It will be certain to be very hard in the
depths of the harsh winter ahead. How will we endure? . . .
Will we endure? But, but – we are forgetting. God has been
with us in the journey until now. Has he not? Will he desert
us now? Surely not! No! He will go on with us. Yes. Yes! Of
course he will. What have we to fear, really? If God is our
support – and he is – who or what can harm us?'

The children were awakened with a jolt. The boat hit the
pebbly beach. They fell forward with the impact and tumbled

into the men in front of them. Willing hands grabbed Justice and lifted him out of the boat, 'Come on, youngun, come on, youngun!' His feet were instantly plunged into the icy water, up to his ankles. The numbing pain shot up his legs. His sister stood beside him. They grasped each other's hand. Together they stepped out of the ocean on to dry land.

Continuing to hold each other's hand, they slowly walked a few faltering steps up the beach away from the sea and towards the dark woods. The snow fell gently upon them. They heard the muffled gabbling of the men making fast the boat behind them. They heard the pounding, incoming waves followed by the sucking scrabble of the receding water as it raced back over the pebbles. The children stopped and looked at each other.

'Justice, our adventures are over, now,' said Prudence quietly.

'Over?' replied Justice. 'Over? I should think not. Why – they've only just begun!'